Music Is the Key

...Music Lives in Me

By Leslie Guity

Edited by M. Malaika Adams-Minor

BK
ROYSTON
Publishing

BK Royston Publishing
P. O. Box 4321
Jeffersonville, IN 47131
502-802-5385
http://www.bkroystonpublishing.com
bkroystonpublishing@gmail.com

Cover Design Art by: Anissa Lorena Moore
Cover Design Layout: BK Royston Publishing

ISBN-13: 978-1-951941-02-4

Printed in the United States of America

Dedication

This book is dedicated to my family and close friends who stuck by me and became family.

To the single parents everywhere struggling to parent their children, teach them in the way that they should go, to keep a roof over their heads and food in their children's mouths, I see you. And you are not alone. Whatever you need is in you.

God lives in you and me. And my testimony is that music lives in me.

Acknowledgements

First and foremost, I'd like to acknowledge my family because family is everything and because of them my life is rich with love, culture and music.

Through ups and downs we still stick together: Papi and Mami, Ruben, Renan, Paula, Tania and Rona.

Then there are my children who kept me on my toes. I call them my Loves 1, 2, 3, 4, and 5: Tierra, Anissa, Kayana, Noah and Taylah. Love #1 gave me beautiful intelligent grandchildren: Derrick Jr., Aubrielle, Kayleigh, and Isaac.

God sends angels to help me through life. There are friends who became my sisters who came in my life and stayed there. They are Gina Fernandes, M. Malaika Adams-Minor, Valjeane Thibodeaux and Breggette Thomason. I have been friends with Gina for 40 years plus and we never skip a beat. These ladies have been knitted into my quilt. They show up when I need them most and vice versa.

There are also: Sharon Campbell and Jonathan Singleton, amongst others (Maria, Maggie, Miatta, Lerato) who God sent to impact my life and still active in my life.

God, through my daughter, had me meet Pastor Roland Cooper and Sister Pat who introduced me to Christ by their walk with HIM. I also want to thank Della Saunders for being my prayer partner for years tearing down strongholds, praying for the sick and watching them recover, praying for each other and watching our lives change for the better.

I want to acknowledge and thank the ones who believed in me and my work and contributed to the funds of publishing this book:

Marcine Ricketts
Lorena Baker Roberts
Tania and Rona Guity
Patricia Dawson
Kharlita Walker
Gina Fernandes
Pastors Phil and Ingrid Tucker
Wilbur McBride
Bernadine Kirkland
Wanda Michelle Grady Reynolds

I want to thank the ones who read this book to get encouragement and critiques to see if the book would appeal to a broader audience. I truly appreciate you. I couldn't have completed this book without you.

They are:
Christine Tangishaka
Diana Cooper
Milan Minor
Tricia Jordan
Anissa Moore
Taylah Guity Moore
M. Malaika Adams Minor

And last but not least I really appreciate my colleague Regine Boursiquot who lunches with me listening to my rants, jokes, hearing my songs and watch my creative mind go round and round daily.

Thank you, thank you , thank you.

Table Of Contents

Introduction

It took me years to write this book. Fear was one of the factors in how long it has taken me to fulfill this vision. What am I afraid of? Am I afraid of facing my past, dealing with previous hurts and experiences? I understand that I have been delivered from my past, and that I am a new creation in Christ. Fear does not live here anymore.

There were other obstacles I had to overcome. I was making myself busy with life's challenges. The computer kept catching viruses. I had to literally start over twice. I, also thought I was doing God's work by singing in the choir all of these years. I probably was doing God's will at first but wasn't doing the main thing that he was asking me to do, which was to use the other talents he gifted me with.

It's also a challenge for me to stay focused; having attention deficit. When writing this book or a song, I receive information in parts like a puzzle. Therefore, I have to put the parts together, which takes time. Laziness was another factor in not getting this book done until now. But as I write and put my account on these pages, I am getting excited to share my story.

So here goes…

Welcome to my Memoirs with a twist. In my life I went through ups and downs but God was there all along speaking to me in a language that I understood… Music

I am writing to share, to encourage, to motivate you to live life to its fullest, utilizing your passion as an outlet and a flashlight to illuminate your path.

Let your praise be your umbrella to shield you from the storm…

I invite you to visit my journey ….

Have a nice trip!

Let Me Introduce Myself!

Let me tell you a little about myself. I was somewhat of a tomboy. Okay, I was a tomboy. I used to cut my hair and roll up the sleeves on my jacket. I wore cat glasses, which were the thickest ever; one might call them bottle caps. I was teased a lot and called four eyes because of my glasses and the fact that my last name was Gudry, or should I say (greedy). These days, I now believe that teasing would be classified as bullying. Though, I was bullied I still strived to be myself.

I am a true extrovert. I can't go anywhere without meeting people; sometimes even befriending them. I talk to anyone, even strangers. I love to compliment people; especially their clothing style. I love to encourage folks to be the best they can be. I know a lot of people. Many flocks to me; sometimes all at the same time. I have been told several times to run for mayor. One of my nicknames is Govnah.

My favorite color is orange. I think everyone on earth knows that. I have nicknames such as Orange lady, Lady Orange and Orange Queen. When I ordered pizza and the delivery guy who I didn't know said, "Thank you Ms. Orange" and mind you I didn't have any orange on, I guess my reputation spoke for itself. Even so, my second favorite color is baby blue, but lately I have been wearing mint and army green.

I love making people happy. I love making them laugh. I love telling corny jokes like," What is the banana's favorite gymnastic move? Banana split." I have a lot more. I will tell them in another book. I love long walks and sitting by beaches or lakes. I love playing pool, swimming in a pool, bowling, and shooting 3s in basketball. I love watching basketball and football games and am a true Celtics and Pats fan. I love church mints, and can eat a whole bag by myself. I binge watch Hallmark movies. I love playing solitaire. I can play it all night without sleep. I'm addicted to Wordscapes and had to delete the application off of my phone because I played that more that I tended to my responsibilities. I love making up words which I will be doing throughout this book. I love to write songs and poetry, and drawing stick people. I hear songs in my head and record them on my phone so I won't forget them. I love to sing…nothing makes me happier.

Nevertheless, I have been through a lot during my life. I was a sickly child and had my mother regularly in the hospital. When I caught a cold, I couldn't shake it. I was born with curvature of the spine (scoliosis) and later developed RAD (Reactive Airway Disease), which is a form of asthma. I am currently taking medicine for high blood pressure and a host of other issues.

I was told by doctors that I could not have children because I was sickly. I was also anemic. At one point, they said I had G6Pd blood deficiency; whatever that is. Oh, and when I had my menstruation cycle, I would bleed to the point of hemorrhaging. I fooled those doctors though, I didn't have 1 or 2 children, I had 5 children.

I am a worshipper and prayer warrior. I find every opportunity to pray …Prayer works. My worshipping God is another reason I am writing this book. I am just describing a little bit of my personality for you to get to know who I am.

Now that you have some facts about me, we can continue the journey…

Born In The USA

My parents were born in Honduras. My father came to America to find a place for his family in 1964. Then he brought my mother and two older brothers Rudolph and Renard to join him in 1965. They came to the United States to make a better life for themselves; to live the American Dream. I was born prematurely in August of the next year in Boston City Hospital; on American soil. I guess you could say I was their "Welcome to America" baby. Maybe that is why I like the movie "Coming to America" so much, hahahaha. Well, back to the story.

My father worked as a mechanic and was also a musician by night. My father can fix anything. My mother worked as a factory worker making baby bumpers for cribs, and later drove for school transportation. Bringing up a family in a new environment could not have been an easy feat.

I love each and every one of my siblings…. Rudolph was the oldest and protective one; he is still protective. No one could mess with you when he was around. He is a musician and has a voice that he can use for voice overs. Rudolph is also very intelligent. I remember helping one of my kids write her paper when she called my brother who gave her all this knowledge that was in his head. Information was complete with numbers like how high a specific building was, how many floors the building had, when it was built, etc. He was truly thorough. We were in a band called Masterwork, then MW2. Later, we changed the name to Excel together. We were good; I mean really good. We shouldn't have given up or we probably could have been millionaires by now. We did cover tunes as well as original music that people liked. We gigged all around Boston and the surrounding cities. Through this band, we developed new family members such as Nat, Giana, Alison, Raquel, Darlene, Kane RIP, Trent RIP, Ward RIP & Germain RIP to name a few…brought together by music. I call this brother Big Bro Almighty or Rubbin or Rubbincito.

Next, is my engineer brother Renard who was and is soft spoken. He is also intelligent to the point where I call him for every electronic need. We went to school together for some years. When we walked together, I took three steps for his every one step. He used to yell at me to hurry up. Teachers used to compare me to him. I told them, "I don't even know what he is talking about when he speaks. He used to take apart all electronics and put them back together again. Who does that? He took all different types of math. He graduated a valedictorian from high school. He was an A student and I was a C my way-out student… I call him Naner or Ugly.

Our family grew. A year after I was born, my sister was born and then eight years later the twins were born. I became the eldest girl and the middle child. My sister right under me…she is tall talented and beautiful. I remember when she passed me height wise. She does her own hair, which looks like it was styled in a hair magazine. She makes clothing and has made several of my outfits when I sang at weddings, during my pregnancies or just going out with friends. Whenever we were going out to a party, I would

2

have to wait for her to make herself an outfit. Growing up we used to fight like cats and dogs but we get along now. We are learning how to agree to disagree. I love hanging out with her. We love music and basketball and joking around. I am proud that she graduated from college while going to work and tending to her daughter at the same time. I love this sister Nonena or Patrice.

My parents, my two brothers, my sister, and I lived on the corner of Paloma Street and Blume Hill Ave. in the 1970s and then my parents bought their first home on Avelon Street where they still reside. We call their home Gudry Central. Our parents spoke two languages, neither of which was English…Spanish and Garifuna. They managed life English-less (if this is a word). We learned English in school before there were bilingual programs. Though my parents didn't speak English, I can't remember ever speaking in Spanish. Communication was interesting.

Eight years after my sister the twins were born, came my, my generation leg bracelet, Tasha. She is a twin. If you look at old photo albums Tasha is never far from me. She is the sailor mouth of the family, but she's working on it. We spend most of our time shopping, eating seafood, and watching movies. She drives me everywhere. She has a lot of insight. She doesn't take any nonsense; especially from her children. She is a passionate person and people think she is mean. This lady can do anything she put her mind to, such as fixing a car or designing a bedroom. I love that about her. I call her Tani or Tangee.

Her twin, Ronel is my Nona. I didn't think the girl spoke, but when we do speak, we talk about life challenges and triumphs for hours; and she makes a mean potato salad. She is a major introvert. She is a promoter, bartender and ticket master to name of few of her 100 jobs. Though her jobs cause her to socialize with big groups of people, she would rather stay alone in her cocoon.

Tasha and Ronel were my experience in teenage-ism. I will never forget when their friend came over a little before their curfew. He had a car, so I said that they could go buy some food and come right back. I sat on the porch for hours, 5 hours to be exact, waiting for them to return. The guy claimed that his car broke down. I told that guy its best he goes home now before I explode. The twins were on punishment for rest their lives. I was supposed to give them money. I kept my money. They were probably preparation for me when I had kids.

Like I mentioned earlier, my father was also a musician from whom I got my love for music. He played alto saxophone and piano and he was the first operatic voice I ever heard. My brother is also a musician. My uncle and many other cousins are or were musicians or deejays. I used to go down to the basement and listen to their rehearsals and sometimes not go all the way down, but sit on the stairs next to the basement door. Get where I am going with this? We Gudrys are musical. Music is in our DNA.

Mami used to dress my sister Patrice and I the same since we were only one year apart. Every Sunday she would dress-up all of us complete with dresses for the girls and dress pants and collared shirts with suspenders and bowties for the boys. She even made dresses and short sets for my sister and I. She made a living as a seamstress in Honduras.

4

Music Is The Key

We grew up eating fish on Fridays. One time we ate steak on that day by mistake and we thought we were going to hell, Lol. We could only go outside after we finished our homework. As soon as we got home from school, we had to put on our play clothes. I had to practice typing at least 15 minutes daily. We had all sorts of educational resources. We had encyclopedias and other educational resources to help with homework. Back then there was no such thing as Google or internet. We played games such as Atari where the ball went back and forth ever so slowly. We had toys like phony bologna and jacks and baby alive. We played games outside such as old lady witch, freeze tag and kick and punch soccer. We also played football and baseball. We were pretty much latch key kids. During the weekdays, Papi worked during the day and Mami worked nights; then she switched to days. When both of our parents were not home, we would wait until right before they got home to do our chores. On the weekends, Papi used to wake us up at 5 am because he said that night time was for sleeping. We had to do our chores which included fixing our rooms, cleaning kitchen, washing clothes at the Laundromat and the like. I remember one day my sister and I were cleaning our room and a song came on…we started singing the song and laying on the bed. My mom came in and yelled at us to finish cleaning. It was funny.

We are blizzard of 1978 survivors. We were jumping from the second-floor porch into the heap of snow below. We were also playing Hide and Go Seek. The snow was so high it was easy to hide. We had to walk miles to the grocery store because you couldn't drive. I even found a one hundred-dollar bill in the snow.

We always had family living with us; aunts uncles and cousins. I had a cousin named Brennan. He was so mean. One time our dog Penny came upstairs and ate out of his food when he went to answer the telephone. I tried to tell him that the dog ate out of his food, but he threatened that he would hit me if I interrupted him while he was eating, so I watched him eat his saliva filled food. After he licked his fingers, he asked me what was I trying to tell him. I said" The dog ate out of your food." I reminded him that I tried to tell him but he would not let me speak…Hope he learned a lesson.

The neighbors on our street were like family. My parents used to take us and some of our neighbors to beaches, parks, etc. It was a fun time! In fact, most of them are my social media friends right now. One of the neighbors taught me how to ride a bike. We also went to school with them. The school system sent our whole neighborhood to the same schools. I had a great childhood.

Well-Schooled

Why did I go to so many schools? Only God knows.
I went to several schools during my life. I attended Harrison,
Apricott, Halborn, Courtland, Brennan, Whatley, Westie
(West Rugby High School), Millard Park, Boston Corporate
School, Rugby Community College and UMass Boston.
You can say that I am well-schooled (if that is even a word).
I went to K2 at the Harrison; I went to grade 1 at the Apricott
and attended the Salvation Army after school Program. I
went to Halborn for grade 2 during the bussing era, but ended
up at the Courtland for grade 3. Teachers received a culture
shock back then when they threw Black students in with the
Whites. That was an interesting time for us because we did
not understand what was going on. Then I attended The
Brennan for 4th and 5th grade. There I learned lots of music.
I remember some of the songs we sang back then. I sang a
solo in a concert, but I was standing behind the choir. Stage
fright was real. I ended up going to Phyllis Whatley for middle school with my brother Renard. That school was academ-
ically challenging. I got into many fights there as well, with
young people who thought they could push me around. I had
a fight with a girl because I sent a chest pass to her in a basketball game and it hit her chest. She grabbed my hair while
I was punching her face. Then another girl wanted to fight
me over a boy. I didn't want her boyfriend. We were just
friends. I had a fight with a boy who hit me. I told him don't
do it again. Then, I picked up a table and hit him with it. I
remember I had to talk with my French teacher in the hall. I
told her," For some reason we don't get along but I would

7

like to learn French, so please teach me." After that conversation, she taught me and I learned.

I took up violin, so I know how to play it a very little bit. I also took industrial arts. I thought I was pretty good at it. We played soft ball. I got in trouble because I hit the ball out of the school yard and we had to go inside. Oops!

For ninth grade, I went to West Rugby High School. Westie was fun! Education was easy, except for Science. I kept getting a C in science. There was a riot at the school that year. It was crazy. Teachers got punched out. I only went there basically part-time, because I went to work right after school. I worked part-time at Lewis Shoes selling orthopedic shoes over the phone for residents in nursing homes. Next thing you know, I was at Millard Park high from grades 10-12 with my brother Rudolph and later on my sister. I took a typing test and typed so fast that I was told by the teacher that she would give me an A, and to go find another extra-curricular class to take. In turn, I was in JROTC (Junior Reserves Officer's Training Corps.) instead.

I loved being in chorus class with Mr. Dillard. I sang "Killing Me Softly" at a show in front of the whole school. I also sang "Mr. Postman" and "Beachwood 4579". I was so scared that I was shaking so bad, I could not even put the microphone on the microphone stand. He had to threaten to fail me to get me to sing. When you sang the note wrong, he would slam the piano lid down and yell, "NO NOT LIKE THAT, LIKE THIS !!!" and then attempt to give you the note with his lip pointing to the sky…lol. Mr. Dillard bought the best out of me. High school made me fall more and more in love with music and singing. Much thanks to Mr. Dillard

8

for threatening me out of my comfort zone and making me sing in front of many.

I enjoyed getting to go down to Cape Cod to sing, and staying in what seemed to be a log cabin. I loved singing at Faneuil Hall as well as singing in the Metro Pathways, a music program in the 1980s where we were pulled out of school for one day a week to sing songs like, thank you for letting me be myself again. I was also picked to sing in the All City Chorus. We were asked to sing around the City of Boston. I was always marked constructively present when I was sent out of school to do shows. And in geometry, if you missed class you were lost...and I still graduated with 105 points. At that time, you only needed 95 points to graduate. I basically sang my way out of high school.

Following high school, I went to Boston Corporate School for one year and found it wasn't my thing even though I learned some skills from there. I met some people there; one whom I now work with. For some reason I never got the concept of shorthand, so I transferred to their sister school Rugby Community College. There I took Algebra with an African professor who I did not understand. I got a D+. I was not pleased with the grade, so I took it over and guess who I got as a teacher and guess what I got as a grade ... same teacher and a D+. I kept having to carry my transcript because for some reason the school system kept aborting my records. I eventually graduated from RCC with an Associate's Degree in Business Management.

I furthered my education at UMASS Boston, where I obtained my Bachelors of Arts Degree in Human Service Management. I did not get my Bachelor's degree until 10 years after I started school due to a growing family. Can you tell I loved school? I would have attended more school if it wasn't for the 5 children I had along the way, starting as early as my second year in college at the age of 19. I got my Bachelor's with 4 children, working full-time with the help of my father who watched the kids while I went to class or wrote papers on his computer. He used to say" You got to get that paper" (referring to the college degree) in a Spanish accent; so, I did. Thanks, Papi. I even attended St Patrick's church and took Bible classes in Spanish.

I was the only dark one there, but they didn't treat me like an outcast. I only spoke a little bit of Spanish but I did understand the lesson being taught.

I also attended Elma Lewis School of Fine Arts as an afterschool program, where I learned how to dance, took drama, sewing and music classes, and sang in Black Nativity; a Christmas story written by Langston Hughes, starting at the age 9. We also took discipline classes with Elma Lewis herself. I learned a lot from her. There, is also where I developed the love and appreciation for music and the arts and enhanced my musical skills. This experience shaped who I am as a worshipper…a writer of this book, poetry and songs and jokes. I met lots of people there as well. I also learned fundamental things like being on time.

I find it unusual that I attended so many different schools. Don't you?

The Fine Arts School Experience

Attending Elma Lewis is where I met a lot of cool kids. We took art, dance, music, and drama. My mother made sure we participated in different programs to keep us off of the streets and out of trouble. I remember taking ballet with Ms. Brown and African ethnic dance with Mr. Howard. We also learned the basics of tapping. We had music class with Mr. Ross and Drama class with Mr. Blackman and Mr. Matthews. We had art with Mr. Rivers and sewing with Gus & Lucy. We were also taught how to play recorder by Ms. Brooks. I still have mine and I am not going to tell you how old I am. There were other teachers such as Voncille, Emerson, and Ms. Hillman who poured into our artistic young hearts. The arts connected us.

We learned valuable lessons at Elma Lewis School, everything from black history to respect and esteem. For example, if you came to dance class without your leotard and tights you danced in your undergarment. If you were in a performance and you messed up, you were to keep going and don't let anyone see the dismay in your face, keep smiling. Ms. Lewis demanded the most from us. She didn't want to have children coming out of her care going to jail. She wanted us to be successful in everything that we learned and in everything we did. We learned to work together. We learned how to be on time. I am happy that this school was part of my life foundation.

There was a singing competition and I was late for the audition. After all the auditions, Mr. Ross picked another singer to go to the competition and represent the Elma Lewis School of Fine Arts. After the audition, he took me in the meeting room and explained to me that though I was the best one, I was late and therefore I could not go and represent the School. He also said it would not have been fair for the others who were on time for the audition. Now I can't stand being late.

You can ask my children. I am on their backs about timeliness. Some of my kids can't stand that I make it a point to be on time. Most times I get to a destination and have to wait on others. There is a benefit for being on time though…They say, "The early bird catches the worm!"

During Black history month we marched through the hallways singing "We're gonna march into Boston in the morning Lord" or "WE shall overcome." The school is where I had my first encounter with theater. I was in a play called "The Frog Prince" and I played the role of a head peasant. I saw the king coming and alerted all the other peasants "Here comes the King" as I was bowing and retreated backwards to allow passage for the King.

I loved to sing at a very young age. I used to sing all the time and my siblings used to tell me to shut up. The Elma Lewis school is when I met my first boyfriend. I had a boyfriend too young. I sang; he danced. I never really understood him. If I knew then what I know now about respect and love, I wouldn't have stayed as long as I did with him. I dated him for seven years, seven long years. I started going with him at the tender age of 13 until I was 21. His name was

Marvin David Roberson who we affectionately called Johnny. He was also a preemie so the nurses nicknamed him that because they didn't think he was going to make it. Sometime during our teenage- years he became a five per-center (a form of Islam).

He renamed himself Rakeem Nacio Aleem. We danced in the same dance group together in a group called Masterwork. We were great poppers and wavers. We had a great group of us who used to go against the best dance groups back then. I stopped dancing with them when they started breakdancing. I was not trying to wipe the floor with my body. I can still do the dances with Tylenol assistance.

We went to Elma Lewis School together. We also attended Millard Park High School together. He cheated on me several times but I still stayed with him; silly me. He had some good qualities. He was extremely intelligent; he would use words I didn't understand. He was also very talented. I loved our conversations (the ones I understood). We talked about everything. I thought he loved me. I found out later that some of the things he told me about himself were fabricated. One time he told me that his mom was dead and then I met her later at Elma Lewis...

Going back to when he would cheat on me. There was a time that we were giving a talent show at Elma Lewis and I had him pick up a friend. They took so long to come back. I later found out they slept together. You guessed it! I still stayed with him. He loved other girls. I caught him with other girls several times and still stayed with him. We did the quit thing and then get back together thing, you know break-up to make-up multiple times. We would do   the petting and caressing thing, but I wasn't ready. He waited. Maybe I was a challenge for him, because I would not sleep with him. I guess he got tired of waiting. I finally gave in to him. He was the one I lost my virginity to. He was my everything; or so my young mind thought.

I was a typical teenager. I smoked cigarettes. I used to lie to my mother and tell her that the pack of cigarettes she found was my friends'. I told her that I was just holding it for her. I don't think she believed me. When I went to parties, I drank Long Island Ice Teas, Slow-Gin Fizz, and Heinekens. I even drank Strawberry Daquiris, and didn't know I was supposed to ask for virgin ones. I got so wasted I couldn't even walk. My friends had to carry me. I even tried weed but it would take about 6 joints to get me high. I didn't like to feel like I didn't have any self-control, so I quit. My whole teenage life consisted of school, work, singing, and Johnny, Nacio or whatever his name was.

Wasn't Ready for Adulthood or Tiana?

At 19 I became pregnant. I wasn't sure if I was going to keep the baby. I made abortion appointments every Friday for a month. I didn't make it to any of the appointments. Nacio said the baby wasn't his. The baby had his head and now has the gap in her teeth like him. He couldn't deny her. Everybody but him took care of me when I was pregnant. For example, his friend Randy used to pick me up from everywhere and he made sure that I ate. Nacio even accused us of being intimate. Randy and I just laughed.

I also had another friend who went to school with me name Quan who used to pick me up, take me to his house, and feed me whatever his mom cooked. We got close. He was the one who told me that I was pregnant. I can honestly say that God has been with me before I was saved because he sent people to take care of me during my first pregnancy. I sent Quan on his way though, because his supposed ex was about to have his baby. I didn't need any drama. I had some of my own drama going on.

I worked for the federal government while in college, then I was laid off because they moved to a different building. My mother having me type for 15 min daily, paid off. I went to Job Search Center and took a typing test. I told them that I wanted to work for the state agency. I applied for a job with the state when I was 8 months pregnant. I had an interview and before she gave me her answer as to whether or not

I got the job, I called the lady and told her that I was pregnant and not fat. She thought I was fat do you believe it? I was pregnant and separated from her father. He was probably scared that we were about to become parents. I was afraid also. When I was in labor, I was playing Acey Ducey (backgammon) with my brother Rudolph and kept beating him. When it was time to go to the hospital, my father drove me. He accidentally ran into the curb. That was the time I really felt the labor pains. We got to the hospital at 6:45 am and we only made it to the labor room. There were women screaming. I told my mother to go out there and tell the screaming women I said "shut up." My first little girl came into this world at 7:01 am. I named my beautiful little girl Tiana. Did I mention I really wasn't ready for children? But I became a parent that day.

I Wrote A Poem For Her

On June 16th a baby was born I named her tiana gudry

When I looked at her, I couldn't believe that she was really my baby

Until this day I am shocked to see that this baby belongs to me

I never expected that I would have a baby as pretty as she.

I was going to name her Tiara, but the lady next door to me in the hospital named her baby that, so I named her Tiana. Her real name which means earth in Spanish. Her father asked me, or should I say, begged me to name her N'Shallah which means *In God's Will* in Arabic. I asked him how to spell it. So, my first daughter is named Earth, In God's will; Powerful!

After I had my baby, I went back to the Job Search Center and got a temporary job in agency typing 1099Gs. I started the new job when my baby was 2 months, and two days after my birthday.

My baby's father and I decided to try to make our relationship work. We went to live with her father. It was very short lived, because I found out he cheated on me yet again. I was packing my stuff to move to my friend's house and he grabbed my arm. I told him to let go and he did not. *I*

17

blacked out. We had a mirror on the wall. I pushed him into it and he was still holding onto my arm. The door came off the hinges. There was a hole in the wall. He was sitting on me and wouldn't get up, so I lifted my legs and he hit his face on the wall. His nose bled on my shirt. I was trying to get a knife from the kitchen. He didn't let me get to the kitchen. My friend Giana had to come and get me from the scene. She was shocked at what she saw. I had to get stitches on my hand which was cut by the mirror. I didn't speak to him for a while, but I didn't want to keep him from his daughter. Even after that episode, we started talking again …well sort of. The baby and I moved in with Giana and her siblings for a short time and then I got my own apartment shortly after.

Following this, the lady I interviewed with months before, found out that I worked in the agency so she offered me the permanent state job. I went from a temporary to a permanent job in one month.

Tiana was powerful like her name. She was and is incredibly smart. She spoke English and Spanish before the age of 1. At her 10th month exam, she told the doctor…"no toce mi bariga." He did not believe that she formulated any words, being that she was too young. She repeated the sentence in English. She said, *"Don't touch my stomach,* I said." Next thing you know the doctor called a bunch of doctors into the room telling them that she spoke more than 3 words clearly.

Kids her age couldn't even relate to her because she was and still is extremely advanced. She was selected to enter the advanced work program in school because she was so smart. When she was 2 years old, she saw a "Hooked on Phonics" commercial which helps children learn their ABC's and 123's and she really wanted it. The toddler called the number from the commercial and gave the representative my work phone number to ask me to purchase the product. The representative called me and told me that Tiana gave her my phone number because she wanted the product. I explained to the representative that the child was 2. Did she think that the child would need their product? She was surprised.

What was I going to do with this beautiful baby? Her conversations were so advanced that you would forget how old the child was. She started singing at a young age; perhaps because I sang while she was in my womb. One time she was singing herself to sleep on the bus. She was singing *I Wanna Rock With Ya Baby* by Bobby Brown. It was so cute. I still vividly remember when she was born. I was determined to do my best by this child. I used to dress her like me. I still needed to find out who I was though.

I went to school. I worked full-time. God blessed me with a village to help me raise my child. My parents played a big part in helping me raise her. She went to daycare with great people. At one of the daycares she went to, her father didn't remember to pick her up and they were about to take her with them for the weekend. That was a stressful situation. She went to another daycare after that, which was in the home of the Coppers. They were saved, Christians, when I didn't even know what that was. She went from the Coppers to Little Leaders with Ms. Neicy and Ms. Willa. They were a great school for Tiana.

Leslie Guity

Tiana lived between my house and my parent's house. She went back and forth to Honduras with my mother. She used to ask me questions I had to think about before I could answer them. I remember her asking me why if Mami and Papi (my mother and my father) sleep in the same bed, why doesn't me and her father sleep in the same bed. I told her that she has her own bed, I have my own bed and her father has his own bed. I was glad when she took that as an answer. She was 2 years old when she asked me that. One time after coming back from Honduras, she did not speak English for two whole weeks, only Spanish.

I went to Honduras for the first time in 1989; August 8th to be exact. I went again in 1990. I got a gold tooth there for thirty dollars. I was rich. Back then the money was 3.67 lempiras for every American dollar. I remember going to a night club when we were down there called Black and White. The soldiers came and my American nephew went to run with the people who lived there, and my cousin told him to sit down because he smelled an American. I was dancing with one of my cousins. I turned around and he was gone. He went running from the soldiers who were trying to get boys to be in the military. We even stayed in a hotel while we were there for seven dollars a night. So much happened in Honduras. I recall my sister continuously waking me up because she was scared. I threw my watch at her because she kept asking for the time. Tiana stepped on ormigas (ants); we had to take her clothes off to get the ants off of her. We ran through people's houses from my uncle's guard dogs. I got sick from eating blue crab and had to drink coca cola and alka seltzer. Then to top it all off as we were coming back from Honduras, we all lit up the bathroom in Florida. Our

20

stomachs were totally upset. Overall, it was a great vacation filled with history on where my family came from.

I did a lot of things with Tiana. I knew she could sing since she could talk. She sang in middle school and in high school at Bay Arts academy. I remember when she told me and the guidance counselor that she did not feel like doing her work. I told her that I didn't feel like working but she had to eat. She told me that I get paid. I told her she was being paid because she had food, shelter and clothing provided to her and was not paying any bills. I regret that because I was in school and working and trying to find myself that I didn't spend as much time as I would have liked to with her. I would get home so late some nights from school, that some nights I could not go and pick her up from my parent's house. She spent a lot of time with my parents. She changed my life. She blessed my life. She was the first child and the first grandchild to my parents. An extraordinary girl she has always been, who has now turned into an extraordinary woman. She is a beautiful psalmist and is very creative.

When Tiana was about two, I got pregnant again. Her father and I were not really together. He was not even really helping me with Tiana at the time. I went to get an abortion and he had Tiana. It was the worse time in my life. I never felt so alone in my whole entire life. After the abortion, I was left in the room on the cold table alone by myself. I would not wish this experience on my worst enemy. When I went to go get Tiana from her father's apartment, they were not there. I waited in the cold hallway, just as I waited on the cold table for two hours for them to come. I was so upset at him, because I felt that he didn't even care that I went through that horrible experience. This situation helped me step back from her father even more. I did not really date much after leaving her father.

In 1991, my cousin Rosanna invited me to the new church in Mattapan. I said ok and went with her one Sunday. It was a great service. The singing was great and up on the pulpit sat Elder Copper. He is the husband of Tiana's babysitter; coincidence or not. Even though it was a new experience, it felt weird and good at the same time. My cousin didn't go to church for the next couple of Sundays, so I went by myself. After that, I didn't go back to church anymore that year.

Why Did I Get Married... *This Is Not The Tyler Perry Movie*

From the pot to the frying pan…

It was just me and Tiana for a while. Then I met him. When I first met Donlee, I met him at a Second Academy in December 1991. I went there because they were having a show and I was going to sing in it. We were attracted to one another and we immediately clicked. When I was introduced to him, he said his name was Donlee. I asked him if that was one word or two words, he said one. He was different. I gave him my number and we talked every day for six months straight. He would call me to say good morning during his work break, to say good afternoon, and before I went to bed to say good night. He told me he was a recovering addict but it didn't bother me. February 7, 1992, '*A Tribute To The Black Woman;*' the show was a success.

During our dating I was trying to quit smoking so I was sucking on blow pops instead. He was a smoker. That was hard. That Valentine's Day I bought him a Valentine's card that read (in the front) *On this day I really want to tell you something…* then when you open the card and it read: *I am really glad I met you.* I thought he was the one for me forever… he moved in with me shortly after he left the rehab house. We decided to get married, or did I force him… that's what he said when we were getting a divorce.

23

During our living together I got pregnant. While we were driving around the state, we were having an intense conversation. Suddenly, I felt a very sharp pain across my stomach. I asked him to pull over. I went to the McDonald's bathroom and think I lost the baby in the toilet at 2 months pregnant. I was bleeding so much that we drove straight to the hospital where they confirmed my suspicion. I was no longer with child. This doctor with no compassion said," I specialize in D&C's." Why would he say that to someone who just miscarried? Donlee started distancing himself from me. This was a sign that I ignored. That was devastating. He tried to be there for me as much as he could but that wasn't much. He was a little distant. While I went through that devastation, I planned for the wedding. We should have planned together… an afterthought that came much later. We were to be married on August 22, 1992. This is when the craziness really began.

Something was telling me that marrying him was a bad idea, but I ignored the signs; all of them. You could say I was very naïve. It wasn't even two months since we got married when Donlee started disappearing. He started going on his drug runs. I didn't know how to handle it. I started going to look for him. I would get in my car and drive around looking for him. Next thing I knew valuables began missing. This is when we mounted the merry go around.

Donlee would go from one halfway house to another to get clean. His drug of choice was cocaine. During his binges, he would tell me that he did not want to get married. I told him that we could get it annulled because we were not married that long, but he said no that he wanted to stay in the marriage and I believed him.

I really thought I could handle the drama. The drama was something I was not prepared for. I believe it was a set-up, because I ended up going back to New Covenant Christian Center. I knew I needed a change; something bigger than myself. One Sunday, Joya Hall was up on the pulpit singing worship. She sang Praise Him and lift him up. I was jumping up and down; I never did that before. I had a jump in my spirit. I knew something had grabbed a hold of me that day and I didn't even realize it until I was walking to the bus stop. The next week I knew I wanted whatever I felt that day. I walked up to the pulpit and got saved. Through the whirlwind of a marriage I now walked with Jesus.

Jesus snatched me from the door of death in November 1992. God always spoke to me through music. Like I mentioned earlier my oldest daughter went to daycare at the Coppers. Elder Copper kept inviting me to church. I told him "No thank you, I am soul searching…lol." I got saved at the very church Elder Copper was trying to invite me to.

After I got saved, I needed more God. The church had a convention. I went and was blessed. Joya Hall was leading worship again and she sang, '*The Battle Is Not Yours, It's the Lords;*' and I was going through. It made me feel better. I did not fully comprehend what the lyrics meant but I knew without a doubt that at that point I had been changed.

One day Donlee, Tiana, and I were in church and the pastor called up everyone who wanted to stop smoking. I didn't smoke that much, so I didn't go up. My husband did and got prayed on. On our way home we stopped at the store for groceries and to buy Donlee a new pack of cigarettes. I smoked one of mine and it was nasty. I smoked one of his new ones and it too was nasty. I stopped smoking. He ended up smoking cigarettes outside in his undergarment He could not get back into the bed until he brushed his teeth. He still smokes today.

I am glad I stopped smoking because I developed asthma. It could have been worse. I could have developed Emphysema. Now, I cannot be around anyone smoking anything or wearing certain perfumes, dust, paint, etc., or I risk having an asthma attack.

We decided we wanted a baby and began trying. This led to arguments where we'd blame each other on how we were not getting pregnant. Finally, we were pregnant. I knew because Donlee, who never got sick, was violently ill. He was throwing up all over the place.

He started back on his binges again where he would disappear for weeks then show back up. I would keep taking him back as he was showing me that he wanted to get better. The merry go round ride was going around and round and round and round and round. I could not get off.

My second child was born…I named daughter #2 Alicia, a 1st daughter for him. I gave her my sister's middle name. (noonie) She is the beautiful reddish-brown haired baby who is the jack of all trades. You would not know her hair was naturally reddish brown because as soon as she learned to do her own hair, she kept coloring it.

Alicia used to suck a pacifier under her tongue and would say coyo coyo repeatedly, as she sucked it. When it popped, she didn't want it anymore. She used to beg us to go to the store and get another one. Her pacifier habit got to be expensive. They were a dollar a piece. She sucked them like someone would smoke cigarettes. We had to wean her off. She cried all night for two and a half weeks straight. We did not cave. She finally gave up.

These days she knows how to do everything from hair to makeup to flooring. She is so detailed. When she does a line up on your hair it is perfection. She can untangle thin chains in minutes. She can put book cases together with no effort. Even in video games she excels beating everyone without a thought. Bowling, she easily gets a strike. She is beautiful and smart. She knows how to dance, sing, draw, paint, make clothes, and on and on and on. She is my introvert. She is always around me sitting on my lap. This child eluded the teachers and I one year, because she was transferred from charter school to public and didn't go to school for 47 days. The only reason I found out was because I received everyone's report card except hers.

The school was so apologetic, because not one of her six teachers called me and said that they hadn't seen my child in class. Once she learns how amazing she is, she will be rich.

My third baby, I named her Kayanu, but the nurses kept calling her Keala so that is what I named her; (kaykay). She is my superstar. I was fasting with church and I kept feeling sick. Alicia was only 5 months old. I called my sister in love in Virginia and asked her what I should do. She advised me to stop fasting and go to the clinic. I went to the clinic and they said," You are with child." I didn't know that I was pregnant, because Donlee was out of the house during that time and I hadn't gotten my period yet, since I was breast feeding Alicia.

Donlee came with me to hospital. As soon as she was born and they pronounced that she was a girl he said, *"Oh it's not a boy...We have to try again"* **while I was still on the table**. The doctor changed the subject by telling me how beautiful she was.

This child was very meticulous and didn't like wearing clothes. She also spoke early. I put a dress on her that my mother bought for her. She said, *"Don't put that dress on me; it's ugly."* She was self potty trained. I put a Pamper on her and she said," Don't put that pamper on me; it's nasty." I asked her if she was going to pee the bed. She said no and never peed her bed. We had problems going number 2. For some reason, she was scared to go. I had to make up a song, to distract her so she could go.

We couldn't keep clothes on her. My father used to tell me the reason why Keala was sickly was because I didn't put clothes on her. I just handed him the pajama. He would put it on her and say, *"Don't take the pajama off okay?"* She would say, *"Okay."* Two-seconds later, the pajama would be on the floor. He'd put in on again, and she would take it off again. She had asthma so bad, I had to have her sleep sitting up. She was in the hospital at 6 months old coughing like an old man who smoked all his life. Today, she sings so well, to think she was born with breathing issues. Soothing to the soul is what her voice is. She is also a dancer. She started teaching dance at the tender age of 12. She also writes music. She will be famous someday soon. I can't wait to see her fly.

Keala was also the family negotiator. Her siblings used to send her downstairs to ask me for whatever it was they wanted. She had a way with words, which sometimes worked in getting what she or they wanted, but sometimes it didn't. I remember when I reprimanded the kids because they broke the new bed that I just bought. My outspoken Keala asked to speak and said" With those big words you use, half the time we don't even know what you're talking about." It was hilarious!

Keala also attended Bay Arts Academy; her sister's alma mater. They auditioned her and she got in with flying colors. I remember going to visit the school for a parent/teacher meeting for Keala. A student came into the office and the headmaster told me to speak with her. That student said that she was bored in English class. I asked her what her major was. She said she was a vocalist. I told her to make a song out of the information she was learning. I further explained that if she made up a song, by the time she was finished writing the song class would be over and she would have learned something. She agreed and left. The result of the parent/teacher meeting was that with the exception of her tardiness, Keala was very intelligent and her talents and gift of song were exceptional.

When she was 8, Keala told me she was moving to New York. After high school, she moved to Connecticut to attend college, then to Philly, then to NY and back to Philly, now back in New York. She discussed coming back to Massachusetts, but I don't think she will do that, and so-far it hasn't happened.

Donlee lived with us off and on. He was living up the street and I went over where he stayed to talk with him.

When Keala was 5 months I got pregnant with my fourth child, Norman. My first boy was born. What was I going to do with a boy; a baller? When people say ball is life, it really is for him. Donlee got his boy. I had to quit the choir in my 6th month of pregnancy because worship was on fire and had me jumping up and down, huge belly and all. When he was a baby all he did was eat and sleep. I remember when I was changing his Pampers, he peed on Keala's head. He loved to climb like most boys. He got stitches in his head when he was about two for climbing up on the bunk bed. We watched *The Lion King* every day for about 2 years. The girls would get upset because they did not want to be subjected to *The Lion King* daily, but that was the only thing that kept his attention.

When he was about 5, I had a party and Norman disappeared. I had the whole party looking for him. We found him 3 houses down the street playing basketball in someone's backyard. He said innocently, *"Look Mom, I can shoot."* He doesn't remember, but I taught him how to defend in basketball. He used to get in trouble a lot because he couldn't stay still. He was suspended for leaving school in the elementary school. They found him outside playing in the park next to the school. This happened again in middle school. He left school and went to the store next door. When he was 8 this boy told me that I am a woman and that I am not supposed to be running the household. Where'd he get this information from?

He eats-drinks-sleeps basketball and still going strong. He shocked everyone by growing up to be 6'2. He is extremely handsome. Norman was always in the gym. He was so good at playing basketball that he was playing in the men's league when he was 10 years old. I believe he is going to be famous as well. There was a time when he had sticky fingers. He took the teacher's phone. They asked him if he had it and he said no. They called the phone and it rang in his pocket. I got one of my police friend's to come and scare him. He told him that he was under arrest. I used to spank the boy when he did something wrong, but that did not work so I changed my strategy. I started having him do 250 pushups by the end of the day or jumping jacks. Sometimes, I used to have him sit in the hallway until I said get up. I even had him walk up and down the stairs until I told him to stop. I believe that punishment strengthened his legs so that he can now dunk. Norman made his first dunk when he was 15 in the Bird Street gym during a tournament. He had the guy flying across the floor.

When my husband was home, he was sometimey. Sometimes he was happy, and sometimes he would shut himself out. I am discerning. I knew when something was not right about him. There was a time when we had parties and people would be having a good time while he was in the bedroom with the door shut. He would only come out to get food. Most times, we were having fun only for him to sabotage it with his big mood swing.

You try to keep it together, but sometimes you feel like you
are in a whirlwind...

I Had A Breakdown

I didn't know how to get out of it. I didn't want my kids anymore. I didn't know how to take care of them. I sat there in the middle of a messy house. I didn't even change the baby's diaper. My mom came over. My father took the kids. Mami cleaned around me. I cried all day until I had no more tears. It was probably postpartum depression. I felt like I could not get a grip on anything and that I was drowning. I didn't eat and barely moved to even go to the bathroom. I was a complete mess. I was on the phone with several people. I cannot even remember who I was speaking with, because I was somewhat delirious. I didn't even remember what the conversations were about. I was trying to call DSS or anywhere I could to put the kids up for adoption. I know a lot of government phone numbers, but for some reason I could not find that particular phone number. It was the wildest feeling.

God sent Lanice who was also going through it herself. She made an appointment for me to see Pastor Betty. I felt totally defeated. My husband had married me under false pretenses. He didn't really like me like that, but since I had means i.e., apartment car and a job he stuck with me. I became the enabler. What was that? It's what I didn't mean to be. He introduced me to the court system, because he would steal to support his crack cocaine habit. I went to see Pastor Betty and she listened to me complain about what Donlee did and did not do. I complained about how he was not there for me and that he was stealing rent money, stereo systems,

33

baby clothes and jewelry to support his habit. She interrupted me. She said, *"I used to see you singing"* and asked if I still sang. I told her that I hadn't sung in a while because I was so occupied with life's struggles and was caught in its whirl-wind. I couldn't get my footing. Plus, Donlee didn't want me singing on the choir anymore, since I had all the kids. I didn't know whether I was coming or going. I was praying but was not hearing any resolution.

This was the first time in my entire life when I real-ized that I was lost and I needed help. Pastor Betty told me to go home and sing in the morning and at night and come back in a month. I did that. Every day as soon as I stepped my foot on the floor I sang and while I was preparing for the next day I sang. Before I went to work, I would play gospel music, but I was really singing with it, internalizing the word of God. I wasn't hiding the word in my heart. I was so busy trying to handle the trials instead of casting them unto the Lord.

Mel my cousin in-law came into the book store when I was looking for worship music to sing. He told me to get Martha Munizzi. Her first cd brought me life. *Say the Name* and *God is Here* were special to me. It helped to lift my spir-its and gather Hope.

When I came back to see Pastor Betty, I was a whole different person. I was full of life. I knew that I needed to sing a new song unto the Lord. I needed to meditate on his Word day and night. I needed to rejoice in the Lord always. I needed to worship. I was still in the trials. I was side tracked. I thought God had abandoned me, because God speaks to me through music and worship. But it was I who had stepped away for my conversations with God. To me, the best songs comes through a combination of the testimony of the pain you endure and God brought you out. Worship is warship!

After that experience, I re-joined the choir, went to rehearsal, and sang three then four services with all my children in tow. I made sure that I sang and worshipped and listened to gospel music no matter what was going on around me, so I could be sure that I heard God speak to me.

After returning to the choir, my husband's addiction caused him to win himself a case. My husband went to jail for two years for larceny and when he came out, I was pregnant once again. I had my period on Sunday. My period ended on Wednesday. He came out of jail and we came together on Thursday. And Presto, I was pregnant. How crazy is that?

When I was pregnant with Tyra, I realized that I did not want to be on the merry go round anymore. It was not getting any better. I was totally exhausted. Deep down I knew my husband didn't love me. I could tell by his actions. He used me for what I had and what I could give him. I tried my best to do my part as a wife but discovered that love can't be one-sided. That would be just like a car trying to drive with only 2 left tires.

The Birth of My Exclamation Point

I had a clinic appointment on July 3rd, and they told me that it was at 1 pm, but we were already there at 10am, so they saw me anyway. I was three centimeters dilated. They sent me to the main hospital. I hadn't eaten. They sent my friend Giana, to get me something to eat. I asked for a steak and cheese sub and she came back a dry turkey sandwich. I was so upset. They probably told her to get me something dry. They induced me at 5 something in the afternoon. There was a male nurse who came in and out of my room with no personality. I had him removed, but not before my water broke and I told him to clean it up. Giana was there supporting me through my labor. Tyra was born at 1:54 am on the 4 of July.

She is genius status...She learned how to play piano by watching Youtube tutorials...Who does that? She makes sure that you know that she is there. She demands attention. She is a straight A student when she stays focused. She is extremely sensitive. I knew she was going to be something else when she was born.

When she was 2 days old, she pulled my shirt so far because she was hungry and she knew what she liked or didn't like at such a young age. I remember putting a shirt on her with quarter sleeves and some capris. She said, *"I don't like these pants and this shirt is too small."*

When Tyra was one year old, we missed her bus, so we took public transportation. We got on the rear of the bus because I was running for it. The bus driver started talking to Tyra who was in the stroller, looking through his rearview mirror. He asked her where she was going and she said, *"to work."* He asked her where she worked and she answered, *"church."* He asked her what she did there. She said, she sings... she started singing *"Hallelujah, Hallelujah everybody on the bus say Hallelujah"* and everybody on the bus said, *"Hallelujah."* The girl had church on the bus. It didn't surprise me when she got baptized. She was so... cute; people always wanted to pick her up. Alicia was picking her up until she was about 5.

She used to tell Norman what to do. She used to tell Norman... *"Mommy said put on your seatbelt."* I didn't say that, mind you. They would always argue. I know Norman was tired of her trying to boss him around. One time they were arguing and Tyra said, *"That is why I am smarter than you."* Norman then said, *"Mommy, Tyra said that she is smarter than me"* and I said, *"Tyra, leave your brother alone"* lol.

Tyra learned how to cook early. One day, I had come home from work and the older girls who were 14 and 15 at the time were lounging in the living room while their 8-year old sister was making breakfast, complete with pancakes, sausages eggs, and home fries. There was a time when I heard arguing and found out that Tyra was the one who cooked the food, I asked Alicia to cook. Alicia promised Tyra could wear her shirt if she cooked. Needless to say, that didn't happen.

Love her like cooked food. When this child is mad though and things don't go her way, she would slam things and leave… She gave me a run for my money.

I don't know where I'd be without these kids who kept me and still keep me on my toes, praying for their well-being.

Praise the Lord, O my soul. I will praise the Lord all my life. I will sing praise to my God as long as I live.
Psalm 146:1-2

Saving My Marriage?

My husband had his own set of problems. Though we had a connection, his ultimate goal was to have somewhere to stay when he came from his binges. I knew, because one day we had a conversation and that is exactly what he said. I believe he was looking for his ex-girlfriend in me. She was Hispanic, wrote poetry, and had a nurturing spirit like I do, but I wasn't her. I was and am me.

We spent a lot of time apart. We only spent enough time to make beautiful children. I knew shortly after we married that he didn't want to be married. I should have gotten the marriage annulled.

My husband and I had a meeting with Pastor Copper. I didn't even know where he was to even tell him about the meeting, until he showed up at my door. Pastor Copper's meeting before ours went on a little longer than it should have. This allowed Donlee and I to talk on the top of the stairs at church next to Pastor Coppers office. Our whole relationship we really never got a chance to talk because he was always gone. He was out of the house more than he was in it.

He would go to programs and leave early, then expect to come home and would call me out of my name. I used to say, *"I am sorry you feel that way."* I told him that our marriage was not working. I felt like I was the only one in it. He said he wanted the marriage, then in the same breath said that he didn't want to get married. I asked him again what he would like to do, because I was tired of being in a marriage where I didn't know where my husband was half the time. I couldn't go to singles events because I wasn't single and I couldn't go to married couple events because I did not know where my husband was. We were never in agreement.

I feared that our only means of communication was making love. It reminded me of the song Roberta Flack sang where the lyrics were *"There's more to love I know then making love, and I remember you in making love."* I bent over backwards for this man. I went to AA, Al-Anon and any meeting he needed to go to. I was trying to make the marriage work.

Because of his addiction, there was also friction from my family. They flat out didn't like him because of what he was doing to me. I was trying to stick up for him and all awhile trying to keep my family at bay. There were things that we agreed upon and then he would say that he didn't agree to it and that I forced him. It was so draining. The conversation went on for about an hour. It felt like eternity.

The couple that was in Pastor Coppers office was finally done. Pastor Copper apologized for having us wait that long. After prayer, Pastor Copper asked Donlee the same question I have been asking him for years. He described our situation as being me and the children in the car. I am in the passenger seat and the children are in the back seat. He said that Donlee was standing outside of the car. He said me and children are ready to be a family and Donlee is uncertain.

Donlee did like he always did to make people believe that he was okay and told us what he thought we wanted to hear. He said that he would come visit weekly (he was living outside of the house at the time). He said he would give me $100 weekly, along with several other promises, which were broken. They were probably broken before we ever left Pastor Coppers office.

I called Pastor Copper and I told him that I wanted a divorce. He told me to study about divorce. I read Marriage, Divorce and Remarriage in the Bible. It was very enlightening. Then, I read a scripture in 1st Corinthians 7:15 which says, *"But, if an unbeliever leaves let it be so. The brother or the sister is not bound in such circumstances. God has called us to live in peace."*

That was my cue! In our conversations Donlee would say that he doesn't have God like I have him. He would say things like, "I am not your client" whenever we would talk. I didn't understand what he meant by that, because I didn't have relationships with my so-called clients. I just gave them information that they needed. It was clear that we were unevenly yoked.

His actions said he did not want to be with us. Since he said it several times and then took it back, saying that he didn't want to be married, I decided to help him out one day and filed for divorce in December 1999. It cost all of $162 to get a divorce.

I had to put an ad in the paper, because I did not know where he lived. I had to wait for the mail to come back to me so that I could file it with my case. It never came back. I had to go to Roxbury Post office to have them locate the mail.

They found it in the wrong bin. They gave it to me and I walked straight to the court.

I also had to put an ad in the paper that I was seeking a divorce, since I once again didn't know where he was. I received a phone call from him. I told him about the divorce. I asked where he lived, but he didn't want to tell me. I had to go to court because they said that I would have to take a class called *Children of Divorced Parents*. I didn't feel like I should have to take it, because the children lived with me and he was just an infrequent visitor. This court date was to waiver having to go the class.

I sat in the courthouse with papers from my landlord stating that I was the only one that lived in the apartment with the children. The judge was saying, *"State your name and case"* to everyone who walked up there. When it was my turn, she said, *"You must be Mrs. Morse."* I answered, *"Yes, your honor."* She said, *"The children live with you and he is never around?"* I answered, *"Yes, your honor."* She said, *"Motion granted, have a nice day."* I did not have to take that mandatory class. I did not even have to take out the papers from the landlord. All I could hear while leaving the court room was *"State your name and case, state your name and case."* She called me by name.

The divorce court set a date in July, but I postponed it until September because I just had the little fire cracker baby. That September the 28th, I took a half of day off to go to court. My friend Marissa met me, so we could go together for moral support. Donlee was told the date on one of his infamous appearances. We got there; no Donlee. We listened while this couple was getting a divorce. The judge said, *"You get the vacation house, you get the Maserati, you get the yacht.* "Marissa and I were looking at each like, *these people are rich.*

When it was my turn, the judge said, *"You want a divorce and want to return to your maiden name and you have full custody of the children?"* I replied *"Yes, your honor."* She said, *"Motion granted have a nice day. Make sure you make your way to the Child Support Enforcement Office before you leave the courthouse."* I said, *"Yes, your honor."*

I felt like doing the "Can you feel it!" commercial where they ran, jumped, and clicked their heels in the air or did a cartwheel. I was free! I called my boss to tell him that I was on my way back to work. He sensed my elation, so he told me to enjoy the rest of the day and didn't even charge my time for the whole day. I sang, *"Thank you Jesus."* I sang God's praises.

I tell people when they ask, that I am happily divorced. I met Donlee while singing, while with him stopped singing, left Donlee and I am singing AGAIN.

Home

I had taken the first-time home buyer program in 1998 and received a certificate but never used it. I had gotten a flyer from the Boston Home Center about buying a house. Early 2001 I was having a conversation with my friend Marissa, and in walked Norman. He was 3 at the time. He didn't speak clear English at all. He used to run his words together so we didn't know what he was saying. But this particular time, he didn't even say excuse me he just blurted out..."pack up your things, we are not going to spend another winter here." It was clear as day. Then, he went back to speaking gibberish. I thank God I had a witness who heard him say those words, because no one would have believed me.

I applied to buy a house from the city of Boston. I was number 11 on the lottery list for the house. They called me and asked if I wanted the house. This meant that 10 applicants had fallen through. I told them that I would pray and get back to them. Bishop Thompkin, Pastor Thompkin at the time, was telling his testimony about when he became a pastor. He asked for a sign and it was given to him. I prayed and asked the Lord to give me a huge sign if the house would be mine.

The next day I went to work at 9 instead of 10 because they needed someone to answer phones while they were in a meeting. That year the city changed the one-way street into a two way. I was crossing it to go to work and I almost got hit by a huge Monadnock water truck. The name of the street that the house was on was Monadnock. I got to my desk and immediately called the city and said that I wanted the house. There were signs everywhere. We were driving down the street going to meet the inspector at the house and there was a smaller Monadnock water truck driving slowly right in front of us.

The broker kept asking for paperwork piece by piece. I asked her for all the items I needed so I would not have to keep going back and forth, but she always found something that she forgot to get from me. I had to go from one side of town to the other side and back to work several times.

They wanted to know what size undergarment I wore for as much paperwork as they required. At one point they told me that they could not give me the mortgage. I asked the broker did she know who my father was? My father is God and he told me that this was my house. I said I don't know how you are going to get this mortgage to me, but this house is mine.

She said ok and three days later called me and told me to go to the credit union and see if I could get a consolidated loan, so I did. I was told by the credit union that I was denied that consolidated loan because I had too many outstanding debts. This didn't make any sense since I thought that, that was what a consolidated loan was for. My ex-husband had left me with a lot of debt. I took the denial letter and left the credit union.

Three days later I called the credit union and asked to speak with the loan manager. I was connected to him. I asked him what a consolidation loan was used for. He told me it was used if you had too many outstanding debts. I asked him to look at my loan denial result. He read it and told me he would call me back. He called back and asked when I would like to sign for the loan. I told him that I would be there in 15 minutes.

He apologized for not approving it the first time. I sent the broker the information. Three days later the broker called and said I got the mortgage. After this great news, there were two closing dates that didn't work for all parties before the actual closing.

When they gave me the keys, I went to the house and opened the door and rolled from one end to the other end of the large living room. I bought a house working part-time with 5 children. God gave me the house; no other way to describe it. I said to God that he gave me these children so I needed somewhere to raise them and he supplied the house and I was singing Jehovah Jireh my provider.

And my God will supply all your needs according to the
riches in glory in Christ Jesus.
Phillipians 4:19

Single Parenting Ain't Easy

Single parents go through a lot. They try to keep a roof over heads, keep food on the table, clothes on backs and a full-time job. We try to make sure they go to the doctors, dentists and optometrists. We make sure we get to parent/teacher meetings, field trips, award ceremonies, basketball games, singing recitals, dance recitals and the like.

I was a single parent before I was a single parent. If you own a house, you have to pay mortgage, water, gas, electricity, cable, internet, home phone, cell phone, security system… must I go on. We also have to take time with the kids to talk with them, do extracurricular activities, take them to church, make sure they are up for school, take them to the hospital if they are sick, make sure they have pocket/emergency money, make sure they do their chores and so on. With all that, we still have to make time to stay healthy and rested. This is hard work…we are wired for hard work.

We have to deal with different types of attitudes, other people's children (kids' friends), etc. You have to teach how to become productive and self-sufficient adults in society by teaching them God's word, to cook and clean, and how to manage money. To give, is to receive. I wish that the kids could understand that the things you do for them and try to keep them away from are for their own good.

Being single parent, I had to be creative on how to teach my kids. I would play educational games such as having them spell words. I would give them math problems like

51

1 plus 2 plus 5 minus 3 equals... and they had to give me the answer as quick as possible. I taught them how to play Checkers, Connect Four, pool and to bowl, therefore teaching them how to strategize. I taught them how to play basketball.

Most of all I would teach them about God. Even when it was snowing I would have them reading books and writing a summary about what they read. I would even have them give a sermon if we did not go to church due to weather or illness. We even made a make-shift alter for them to give their own sermons . We colored a big poster board as a family. It is still hanging in my music room.

We had picnics once a year where we could give constructive criticism and tell the person how they felt about them with no repercussions. We would tell what good things happened the year before and what bad things happened. We'd have to state tangible goals we wished to accomplish the coming year. It was a good time. As grown children they still want to continue this tradition.

My eldest daughter joined us one year. She was an adult with husband and children when I first created this tradition. We skipped a year for this tradition because everyone decided that they were grown and all moved out. I was actually home alone for 7 months.

I was actually ok with it because I didn't really have time to myself when the kids were home. Everyone needed something. Sometimes they'd rebel against how I ran my home. At one point I had three children in school, one was a junior in college one a sophomore in college, and my baby a junior in high school. I am thanking God for them and for provision. I love my children and would do anything for them. Thank God for my children and His help, grace and mercy.

Though I am a single parent God sent angels to help raise these kids. I have been trying my best to train them up in the way they should go and the word of God says they won't depart from it. God was always in the mix.

Being a single parent was hard because you had to spread yourself amongst all the children. I can't tell you how many times I heard all my children say that I don't love them as much as I love the other. Each one of the children wanted all of my attention.

I did the best that I could to raise my children to be responsible adults.

For your maker is your husband – "The Lord Almighty is his name – the Holy One of Israel is your Redeemer; he is called God of all the earth."

Isaiah 54:5

Through it all, I sing.

Abstinence While Single

Every time I would tell someone that I am abstinent, they asked how can that be? The year that I got a divorce I was still sleeping with ex-husband and was violently ill. I would get an unexplainable fever of 104. I kept going back and forth to the hospital. I was tested from everything from a virus to HIV. They could not find anything wrong.

One day on July 8, 2001 I was getting ready to give the baby a first birthday party. I was sick as a dog. I still got up and set the party up for the baby. We were divorced and still came together that morning. It was at that point that I decided that, that was the last time that I would lay with him; and my fever miraculously went away. I guess it was guilt that was making me sick.

I was now saved in 1992 and no longer could I do what I used to do. I knew better than to fornicate when I was no longer his wife. Ever since then I was sworn to celibacy until I marry again. I am the type of person that will give my all. The relationship was 95/5 instead of 50/50 or 100/100, but I am also afraid that if I did break my celibacy, I would end up with more children by myself. I am all good with that.

Many Tried To Break My Celibacy

I was talking to this guy for a few months and everything was going well until he said he wanted 2 more children. He said it with passion. I already had 5 children. I immediately said bye to him. There was no one else coming out of me. I suggested that he find a young lady who would love to have children.

It wasn't going to happen…

One time I went to the pizza shop to pick up pizza because the delivery guy was not available. I had a conversation with this guy who was trying to talk to me. I told him that my oldest child at that time was 15. He said that I did not look like I had a 15-year old or 5 children. We got on the subject of sex because he said he has 3 children and couldn't see any of them.

I told him that I was abstinent. He could not believe me. I told him that sex just confuses things. I told him to look at his situation; the children are paying for him fornicating all over the place. I told him he should at least wear a "raincoat" so that he doesn't make any more babies that he wouldn't be able to see. Ironically, it was raining outside.

I told him that I believe that God will send my husband to come find me. He asked, *"How will I know how the guy is in bed?"* I said, *"If God is sending him it will be all good."* Another guy interjected and said that he and his wife dated for over 1 year and did not sleep together. They prepared to get married by buying a house together. They discussed who is going to pay for what, d when they were going to have kids, how many they would have, and how they would discipline their kids. He said they got married and he was very happy. Their bedroom life was great. We ministered to that brother. This whole conversation happened while I was waiting for one box of pizza which should have taken 15 minutes to prepare.

I am glad God sends people to me to pray for them and to give words of wisdom. I have been celibate for quite some time. Therefore, I'm able to give sound advice, being that I have been through things even falling into temptation. We just have to learn to stay with Jesus. Let the Lord lead the way.

We should not commit sexual immorality, as some of them did and in one day twenty-three thousand of them died.

1 Corinthians 10:8

I went on a date with my friend Pressley. Since I was in the habit of walking everywhere, I told him that I would walk to his house. When I got there, he answered the door in his robe, he looked as if he just got out of the shower. That was fine. I sat in his living room and he went to get changed. He had a bay window with several beautiful exotic plants. I commented on them and next thing I knew, he came out in his Fruit of the Looms to give me a description of the plant. He looked good. He went back to finish getting dressed and we proceeded to our date. We went to the Colonnade Hotel and had a great breakfast. Then he dropped me home. He asked what was wrong, but I couldn't speak on it right then. I was dropped off and went inside the house. He called me and asked again what was wrong. I told him that I felt violated because he knew that I was celibate and that I am waiting for my husband to find me. He said that it would not have bothered him if something happened between us, but I minded. I told him that I felt he disrespected me and he immediately apologized. I decided to give him the benefit of the doubt and we went out again.

This time, I came to his door extremely late so he would be finished dressing. This time, he was already in his car waiting for me. Lol... Pressley and I have history together. I met him at work when he was interning while he went to MIT. We went on several dates. He took me to places I would not have normally gone to. We went to eat at Newbury Street, sitting on the floor eating with chopsticks in high end restaurants where it was 40 bucks a plate and they gave you a tablespoon worth of filet mignon. We were supposed to be an item but we never made time to see each other, because we both were busy. He did everything for his mother which was admirable. He would call me and we would only speak for like three minutes before he had to go. His mom used to say he wasn't there when you could clearly hear him speaking in the background. I had to end the relationship on the bus on our way to work. We used to have some interesting conversations. He never came out disrobed again and I appreciated that, but I still decided to distance myself from him because he swore too much.

There was another guy whom I came close to having relations with to the point of nudity but then I heard a voice tell me to get up. I heard it again, *"GET UP"* ...so I repeated what I heard and told him to **"GET UP."** He said, *"What?"* I repeated what I heard *"GET UP."* He did, though he was very confused. He got up, got dressed and that was the end of that relationship or whatever that was. He didn't even stay friends after that episode. It was very awkward every time we bumped into each other. Avoidance was real. This guy is the one who told me my ex-husband had gotten remarried because he took the job that my ex-husband left. Donlee didn't tell me or his children that he was getting married.

I gave my number to this other guy who worked at Home depot. I don't even know how we got onto the sex subject, but I told him if sex is what he eventually wanted that he was knocking at the wrong door. I told him that I will break my celibacy when I am married and only when I am married. He didn't believe me. He claimed that he slept with people who went to my church. I told him that may have been where they were in their spiritual walk, but I am not the one.

Maybe being inappropriately touched when I was young may also play into the decision to stay abstinent. To date I am celibate, not sexually active, and I am believing in

God that he will send my husband to find me. And no I don't feel like I am missing anything. I am not longing for sex. I would like a love marriage relationship, not sex. I feed my spirit worshipping and singing praises unto the Lord. I starve my flesh.

Looking For Love In All The Wrong Places

If you have a relationship with or get married to someone and there is no love, you will be miserable. You should not be unevenly yoked. Where there is love, the relationship will last. Love conquers all. From past relationships, I have never experienced this love.

Let's talk about Damon. I met him at my cousin's party when we were 10 and 11 years old. We talked on the phone and had great conversations. I remember the day he told me that he was going to prison. He never told me what he did but I used to go see him in prison. He didn't like how my first boyfriend was treating me. One time they even almost fought. I told them if they fought, I was not speaking to either of them. I used to talk to him on the phone in the middle of the night, hiding in the pantry. Back then, the phones had long telephone cords. I guess you can call what we had young love. We used to create the person we would like to see each other with if we didn't end up together. I hope that his wife was who I created her to be. He was dear to my child heart.

I got busy with life and I stopped going to see him in prison. I got a letter from him one year after several years had gone by. He told me that he was getting out of jail and that he had gotten married prior to his release date. At one point, I called myself waiting for him to get out. He was in

63

for many, many years. Yes, yes it was an unrealistic expectation because I was living in the world and he was living in an institution.

I ran into him a couple times since he got out. We just said, *"Hi"* and kept it moving. I ran into him again at the Bay Jazz Festival and he said that I would always be his girl... Next.

I met Royce at Boston College camp at the age of 12. We talked and talked and talked and talked. All the neighborhood kids went to the camp. We played all different types of sports such as tennis, track and of course basketball. I was point guard and received a trophy from them. Many years later, I ran into Royce on the bus. We reconnected. He would come over my house and would not leave until 1am.

I braided his hair. We took the kids to the park, shopping and out to eat. He came to church with me. There was a time when I hadn't seen him for about 2 weeks because of his job. He called and said that he missed me, but he didn't know when he could see me. He asked if it was raining outside and when I went to look out the front door, he was standing there in the rain. That was sweet.

We even prayed together. One day he came to my house and he said that he needed to pray. I prayed with him and all of a sudden, I could not stand so we fell to our knees and I also could not speak English. I was speaking in other tongues and could not stop. I then started rebuking and binding and loosing and casting out lies & deceit, telling them to get out. After that day, I barely heard from him. Then he said that he needed space because he was still mourning a wife who had passed a year before. I told him to take all the time he needed. Deep down I knew he was running. The prayer time was so powerful. It kind of freaked me out as well.

One of my colleagues told me that he got married. Before I knew of this information, I had sent him a sweat suit via mail for his birthday. He received it around the time he got married. .I called him and congratulated him on his nuptials. He asked who told me, and I asked him why he didn't tell me. He claimed that he didn't want to hurt me. I asked him if he loved her. He said she was a nice girl. I'd still take that as a no. If you love someone, you want the world to know, including me.

He called me one day when I was doing worship at church. I answered the call in between services. He asked me if he got a divorce if I would marry him. I said absolutely not. I am not a second thought.

One day he came to visit me and we were standing outside; two drunk men were walking down the street and one of them walked up to me and said, "I was *so fine*." He then said to Royce, "*Sorry, I didn't mean to disrespect you and your wife.*" Royce said, "*she is not my wife.*" The drunk guy looked surprised and said, "*If you ask me, she should have been your wife.*"

Royce admitted to me that he never had a relationship like ours. There was no kissing, no petting, it was just a time of getting to know each other and spending time with one another. We prayed together. We had bible study together. This lasted for nine months. We had great conversations as if we picked-up where we left off when I was twelve and he thirteen. This was intimacy. I wonder if me being abstinent had something to do with our separation. He knew we were not going to have sex if I was not married. I remember Keala used to be in the Boston Children's Chorus with his step-daughter. She told her that she knows her step father because he was at our house every day the prior year. Why did she tell the girl that?

I was so... upset that he got married but one of my choir member friends said that she didn't know why I was so upset when I was the one who prayed him out of my life by binding and loosing all that was not like God. From that point on, I moved on. Some people look for love and then when they find it, run from it. This is what he did.

Before Royce there was a guy named Wilmer. I went out with him to make my first baby daddy jealous, but he actually became my good friend. Even when I was married, he would be there to pick up the pieces of my broken heart. One day, he came and got me from my house. He let me sleep in his bed and he slept on the couch. I am not sure why we never ended up together romantically. He too got married. He actually brought his wife to meet my parents. When you are friends of the Gudry's we treat you like family. I sang at both his father's and his mother's funeral. I was part of their family. He is my son's godfather. I was blessed to have a friend like him.

I met Jordan while singing with Kuumba, Harvard University choir. He became my keyboard player for 15 years. We did many shows weddings and funerals together and when he could not play for me, he would put music on the cassette tape for me. Even though he was busy, he made as much time for me as he could. After 15 years, we started drifting apart musically, but every now and then we would hang out. He was so good to me. I remember going over his house and when I was leaving, he kissed me. It didn't even dawn on me what had occurred until I got to the bus stop. The next time I went to his house, I brought someone with me. We had fun together.

One day I was sick and went to the hospital. I was too weak to go home on the bus. He made me chicken soup and let me crash at his house while he worked. He called my parents and asked them to pick up the kids. He ran an errand and came back. Then he called a cab for me which the driver came up to his door. He had him drive me home. Because of this good deed, when I had my last child, he became her godfather; and what a good godfather he is.

He came to New York with me when I won a singing contest. We were disqualified because we didn't have any sponsors, which they never asked us to have. The organizers didn't have a hotel room so they had us go sleep over one of their friend's house. We had to sleep in the same bed. The next day we went to the office they told us to meet them at, and when they came told us that we were not leaving on that day. I told them that we were leaving on that day and that they better find money to put us on the bus. I was about to jump some people if they didn't get us a way back home that day. Jordan was holding me back. What an adventure. He too is married. He is still in my daughter's life.

At some point there was Jace, who was an aspiring rapper. I liked him a lot. He was cute and very charismatic, but he was playing for the wrong team. Even though I was not saved back then, I knew right from wrong. He was on the wrong side of the law.

I had an associate who said that her cousin bought drugs from him. One day I asked him to come over…he did. I asked him to dump everything in his pockets on my kitchen table and he did. He had a gun, bags of weed, some pills, and big wad of money. I told him that we could not see each other and he agreed. Even though he was on the wrong side of the law, he had a heart. He didn't want me mixed up in his drama, so we parted ways.

Then, there was this Andreas character, which I wouldn't call a relationship. I think he thought I was stalking him because we would literally run into each other everywhere. It was weird to me also. I would be walking down the street near my house and would turn around and he would be in his car waiting at the red light, or I would get off the bus getting ready to cross the street and he would be right there. Did I mention It was weird? I don't know what he told the First Lady but she told me off and made me feel so small. I was surprised that she spoke to me in such a manner. She even thought I was still married. Did she think I would cheat on my husband if I were still married? Geesh. Anyway, that situation didn't end well. I'm glad it's in the past.

I remember Liston, my twin. We met on the elevated orange line. We were dressed the same. We asked each other's name and we were born on the same day. It was crazy that we hung out. One day he was sick as a dog. I attempted to nurse him back to health and I made sure he got to the hospital before I went to work. We still call each other twin today.

At some point there was Ronald, who I knew since teenage years, who barely wore sneakers. He always had skates on. One day, he climbed my back porch and my big brother told him to climb back down. Then he knocked on the front door and asked my mother for my hand in marriage. My mom told him to come back when I was eighteen. It was funny. He too came back around and would come here and make dinner for us. The kids looked at his gourmet hamburgers in horror. There was one time the ex-husband came over while he was over; awkward. They were both seated in the living room, while I was cooking. I served both of them dinner. He would sit and play with the kids, but something was definitely missing from our relationship. He moved on and got married.

I met this guy named Charles at the Gospel Buffet, he and a friend of mine were running the event. He was easy to talk to. We talked a lot throughout the event until a girl came up to me and introduced herself as his wife. Wow! That ended those conversations....It caught me off guard because I thought he was into me as much as I was into him. I shook her hand and said, "Pleased to meet you." Years later he called me to see if I was interested in a business venture. I said I would go meet him, but was never able to make it happen. In the back of my mind, I didn't want to get involved or reacquainted if he was still married. So, I was little glad that our meet up did not pan out.

Lately, he has been liking all my posts on Facebook. I asked if he can pray about and ask the Lord if he would help me get the music out of my head. I have some whole songs some choruses, some vamps and some anthems. He immediately answered yes. Boy did my heart skip a beat. I didn't think I was so into seeing him. Then, one Sunday, he in-boxed me just to bid me a nice day the same Sunday my sister and I decided to go eat brunch. We parked in front of some stairs. Would you believe he came walking down those stairs, right in front of the car beside my passenger seat side window? That was crazy. What a coincidence! That seems to happen a lot to me, where I run into the person I was just talking to or about. I told him he could call me, but he didn't have my number anymore. I gave him the number and we talked about the alleged coincidental encounter. We couldn't believe that we ran into each other after 5 whole years.

I had to find out what year I graduated from University of Massachusetts because I was updating my resume. While looking up the information, found out that Mr. Charles and I also graduated in the same year. Is that crazy or what? He was standing a couple of people behind me. I saw an asterisk beside some people's names. I didn't know what *cum laude* meant. I was just glad to have my name listed as a graduate. It was *Oh Lordie* for me, *"Thank you Lordie."* I wonder if he remembered me from graduation. It felt like I knew him for quite some time. He was supposed to help me with my music which never ended up happening. He wanted to charge me a whole lot of money that I did not have at the time.

One night, Charles was getting ready to drive me home from a shedding session and we were stopped by the police. The cop asked him for his license and registration. He asked the cop why we were being stopped but the cop did not answer. In the meantime, the cop's partner was at my window waving at me. I told Charles not to worry because we did not do anything wrong. I believe we were riding while black. I happened to have on a turban. They came back and asked for my credentials too. I was the passenger. They were not going to find anything on me. I have a clean record. The end result was that they let us go, of course. Charles said a brother is just trying to get some food, Lol. I told Charles that I don't know why he stopped us since he's close to white (Charles is light skinned). He said they stopped us because they thought I had weapons of mass destruction under my turban…lol. We had fun together! He got engaged and is now in his second marriage. I ain't even mad. I knew deep down that he was not the one. I knew it when we went out to dinner and he only gave twenty dollars towards the bill. He was a bit cheap for my taste. Your heart is where you put your money.

Shane

Ever since I was born a Shane took care of me...

My Mami whom I call Dona which is MRS in Spanish, people call her Chon or Shane. The name Shane is short for my mom's actual name since everyone has a hard time with the pronunciation of her name. She bore and raised me. Then when I was in middle school, I had two friends named Shane. When I bought my house there was a guy named Shane who lived across the street and he was a big help for this single parent. He gave me money when I was on my last dime and I don't mean twenty dollars I mean two hundred dollars. He spoke into my son's life about being a man. He was dating his girlfriend for 15 years. I would ask him how long was that for. Every so often I would ask him if he asked her to marry him yet. I know I was being a pest, but he finally did and they finally got married. This Shane was and is like a brother to me.

Now there is this guy who I've had a deep connection with for years, who's named Shane. He doesn't know it, but my nickname for him is Shane Chocolate because he is dark and handsome. Whenever I run into him, it is like no one else is around. We can talk for hours. He encourages me. We used to inbox each other greetings. For example, we would say have a Marvelous Monday, Terrific Tuesday or Wow-tastic Wednesday. I remember the day when I had to lead worship the next day for the first time. I called him up and told him that I was nervous about leading worship.

He said to me very calmly, *"You were born to worship, so just go up there and open your mouth and let God use you,"* and instantly I relaxed because I believed him.

There were times when he literally picked me up off of my feet just to say hi. I asked if he does that to every one of his "girl" friends and he said no, just me. I asked why and he said that I am special. We would bump into each other everywhere like the train station, at the bottom of my street, and even at the Celtics game; and guess what? He was always with a girl. He never introduced them to me as his girlfriend though. It is crazy that I know he is near me without even seeing him physically. I had that connection with the ex-husband.

Even now, there are Shanes everywhere. My mom asked the post man what his name was and you can guess what he said it was…Shane. I went to the Friday's in Brigham Circle for lunch. The waiter came over to me and said, *"Hi my name is Shane, and I will be taking care of you."* He's just another Shane who is going to take care of me. And lately, I haven't even thought about Shane. I guess because I got tired of seeing him with a different woman. I call the new IT hotline at work for help on my computer. A Shane answered the phone 3 different times. I asked if there were any other representatives working with him and he said yes. I bought a phone from you guessed it, a Shane at AT&T store. There is a reason why all these Shane's keep turning up. I don't believe in coincidences.

I saw Shane Chocolate. It had been one year since I last saw him at his church. He came and gave me a hug. I hate that I have a connection with him to the point where I knew he was in the building without even turning around. I prayed and asked the Lord to sever that connection so I can be ready for the husband that God will send looking for me. I was especially happy that his son Daniel recognized me and I haven't seen him for at least 3 years. That made my night. I ran into him at a Gospel concert. I ran into him at my niece's school. Apparently, his son goes to my niece school. I went to a women's conference at a different church and met his mom...I met his daughter and grandson on the train platform within a three-month span. The Lord will make it clear. Or perhaps Shane signifies hope that I will have a husband who loves me for me. I came to a realization that I really don't know anything about Shane. I don't know where he lives. I never actually went out with him. I've never even been in his car. I just run into him every now and again.

We used to speak a lot in person when our children were in the same dance school, then on the phone for a while, but then that stopped. We ended upon a text relationship for several years after that. The hugs he gives me were magical. Every time I think of him my heart kind of skips a beat. That does not happen when I talk with or see anyone but him. I told him by text and he read it; no answer. Trying to force a relationship is like trying to fit a size 10 foot into a size 7 shoe. It won't work. Was what we had considered a relationship, friendship, or just an association; Next.

Confession: Every now and then I still think of him, wondering how he is doing.

Then there is Mr. Conductor Jamal. I first met him when he was covering a shift on the train that I ride. He was smacking his gum. I told him to take the gum out of his mouth and put it on his nose. I would get on the train with my friend Lola. She didn't care for his gum popping. Then, one Sunday he took someone's shift again. He told me his name was Jamal. Everyone else calls him Carl. Well, anyway next thing you know it he was a regular on my train. He would know where I was going based on what stop I got off at. I asked him if he was stalking me and he said yes. He wanted me to sing to him because he found out that I was going to be in a play. One day, I rode the train and I sang to him. He said" Oh, you have it like that? …" I asked him if he goes to church or bedside Baptist with Reverend Pillow and Deacon Sheets. He said" Where do you get the stuff that you say?" He would hold up the train just to talk to me whenever I got off the train. I told him he needs to run the train and he would say that they can wait. I went to Philly. When I came back, he asked for a souvenir and out of my mouth I answered "me." I could not believe I said that to him.

The next time I saw him I told him to forget about what I said. I told him I was sleep deprived. He asked" What did you say?" playing like he didn't remember. He said" Do you mean when you said you are my souvenir." I blushed. He was trying to find out how old I was. I told him I was 25. He asked how could I be 25 if my daughter is in her thirties. I told him" The Guiness Book of World Records." There was another time I told him that I was going to spend time with my sister who was one year younger and he asked how old was my sister. I told him 24. He tried to outsmart me and I called his bluff. My friend passed away. I got on the train and stayed on just to stay in his energy. I was going to go to the end of the line but he told me that they go back to the main station non-stop.

I got off at Fairlawn and ended up at my friend's nail shop and got my nails done. I asked him how he was doing one day and he answered fine as long as he sees me. He said it so loud that my friend that was sitting seats away heard it. One day he was gone. He was transferred to another train. He had given my friend his number but not me. She had given it to me, but I wasn't going to call it unless he gave it to me himself or asked for mine. A couple of months had passed and I ran into him coming up the escalator at South Station. I asked him why he left me. He said that he didn't leave me, they took him away from me. He asked if I missed him and I said a little. His train was on one side of the station and mine was on the other. We held hands at the middle of station then we let go like a scene from gone with the wind. It was the cutest thing. I saw him again. He said that every time he sees me, I mess him up. I asked if I make him stumble and he said yes. I told him I have that effect on people. He was supposed to be making a phone call before he got on his train. He can't use a phone at work. He didn't remember who he was supposed to be calling. The connection we have is unreal. He has yet to ask for my number and it has been about a year. I am not going to hold my breath waiting to see what will become of this. I haven't run into him in a long while. I believe he was really concerned about my age. After all, I am 25 years old with a daughter in her thirties. He is most likely close to my daughter's age. Nothing came out of this flirt fest but I enjoyed the mystery train ride.

I was proposed to three times in my life:

One was a guy named Buddy. He was a security guard at UMass. He said that he was doing big things and needed a partner to share it with. I had just come out of a relationship and was not ready for anything. One was my cousin's baby daddy proposed right in front of Food Market I just laughed. I didn't know at the time that he was my cousin's baby daddy. One was a complete stranger. I told him that he didn't know me. I could be an axe murderer. He was still adamant.

When there are no more words to say there is music.

What is love

Love is patient...I had no patience back then...

Sometimes we have no patience.

And when we don't exercise patience; we are telling God that we don't trust that he will do what He said that He would do.

Love is kind...I used to tell people about themselves without even batting an eye. I thought nothing of it

I love my children...this is I know. They have iPhones and 100 dollars sneakers; I have an android and buy whatever sneaker is on sale. I supply their every need with my last dime.

There are reasons you have to wait; one reason can be that you are not ready yet. Another reason could be the blessing is not ready yet, another reason could be the blessing is scheduled to come i.e., the train is scheduled to come at 2 but you got there at 1. It could be that the scheduled blessing has been delayed i.e. the bus is scheduled to be here at 2:30 but it was caught in traffic and is backed up a whole hour. While you wait you can be doing something productive for instance right now in order to pass the time, I am writing this little insert. I participated in a play. I am writing songs and poetry. I am writing jokes.

While I am waiting on my husband whom God has promised, I will continue to walk in God's will and way. I will worship Him in spirit and in truth. If you want happiness in your life, you can't hurry love or anything else. You can't expect a home cooked meal with a microwave mentality. If it takes a turkey 4 hours to be cooked, you are not going to pull it out at 3 hours and expect to eat it.

IF it is meant to be it will definitely come to pass. IF it, whatever it is, is in God's will and whatever it is, is for you, then it's yours. Sometimes we have not, because we ask not. The worst thing you can do, is doubt for just as faith is powerful so is doubt. God cannot move on your behalf if you doubt. You can't rush God and trust God simultaneously. I heard the Lord say that my husband will not find me if I am still holding on to past relationships. So, I unfriended any guy that I had a relationship with or had a date with on social media. I am moving forward and not looking back. I am working on staying focused on the path that God set before me. Love will find me along the way.

I remember, when I was by myself, I felt lonely but I was never alone. God was always trying to get my attention the whole time. The entire time. God was trying to show me love. I just did not know what it was supposed to feel like.

I have to admit when I was in the relationship with my children's fathers, I didn't really know what Love was. I thought that if you had a connection and were physically attracted to one another, that was love. Boy was I wrong! I had children with two different men and now they are both married to someone else. What does that say about me? I have been looking for love in all the wrong places. I was never loved by a man. I am basically a virgin. It means I had to learn to love or at least what it is. And, I had to learn how to love myself first. I have been saved for a better part of my life and I am just now learned what true love is. Oh well, better late than never, huh? Funny, secular love songs taught me what love was, NOT. Most love songs only talked about jumping in the bed.

When I began singing gospel songs, I didn't know what they really meant. However, when I sang them, I felt liberated. I felt joy and peace. I now realize that they are true love songs. I am just now realizing that I didn't really love the guys like I thought I did because instead of dealing with them I would just throw them out like they were trash on trash day. I would not tolerate foolishness. I was young though. I don't think that I even loved myself that much. I was more like a thinker than a lover.

I would love a real love marriage to show my children what love is supposed to look like. With the ex-husband, I think I liked that fact that I was to be married. I had this painting of what my life would be and just stuck him in it. I noticed that most of the guys that I had a connection with or had an encounter with are now married to someone else, like both of my baby daddies. I learned that though you have a connection with someone, that doesn't mean that person is your husband. I also found that if you are unevenly yoked you will feel the imbalance like a seesaw. The ex was indirectly telling me that he felt beneath me. Once a person puts you on a pedestal there is no longer a relationship, because you can't have a relationship with a statue. Therefore, when you are unevenly yoked, you cannot be yourself. That person with low self-esteem would try their best to dim your light.

I believe that just means that my true husband has not been introduced to me yet. Even though I've been saved for several years, I was trying to get to know God but did not really know him. I now know God intimately. Therefore, I know Love. I know me. I love myself. I love all of my flaws. I learned that if you do not love yourself you should not expect anyone else to love you. So, I will know who my husband will be when he comes to find me.

I am just now in my 50's, starting to understand that there will one day be someone who will love me for me and not try to use me but want to make me happy. There have only been guys who were assignments sent by God to give them my testimony about celibacy and about not settling for less and not having to sleep with someone to get to know them. If you ask me, it only clouds everything. This is probably why they are all married to someone else.

I love...

I love God

I love my Children

I love orange

I love beautiful colors in the sky

I love sunrise and sunsets

I love grapes

I love hugs and kisses

I love to cook and feed people

I love to entertain

I love to crack corny jokes

I love to give compliments (give props where props are due)

I love strawberry ice cream

I love it when children are obedient

I love to sing

Music Is The Key

I love to dance

I love to learn how to play piano more

I love several genres of music

I love to worship God

I love spending time with family

I love to play basketball

I love the ocean breeze

I love swimming (though I am not that good at it)

I love to write poetry

I love to pray

I love watching singing and dancing shows

I love watching game shows

I love to watch sports I love to play solitaire and spider solitaire

I love speaking different languages

I love my grands

I love my parents

I love siblings

I love myself

Did I mention I love God

What do you love?

I asked several married couples who have been married for several years, how did they know that their spouses were the one? Every one of them said that they just knew. Love is not based on how you feel. True love is about knowing. There is no other love like God's love. God is love. God loves you in spite of you. What makes anything magical is Love.

The Start Of The Birth Of My Yayas

My eldest daughter gave me grandchildren. The first one was born in 2005. I was in church when I got the call that she was in labor. I answered the telephone under the chair. I whispered hello and I ran out of Jubilee to the hospital. They thought that I was a midwife and not my daughter's mother.

Darwin is so smart. He got jokes. He loves dinosaurs and doing things like archeology. One day the clock fell in school and he said," I guess time doesn't fly" The whole class was laughing and he got a demerit for interrupting the class. He can play basketball and knows the game very well but only plays for fun. If he did play seriously, he would be NBA material. He is now 14 and almost as tall as my son who is 6'2 and wears a size 13 shoe. He is about to be a freshman in high school. Can you believe that? He is going to some type of scientist, archeologist, zoologist or something up that alley.

I have been taking the public transportation for most of these children's lives. I went car shopping in 2006. I had $2,500 to spend, which I had saved up. I went to different car lots but the cars were so expensive. This is a big feat. Everyone knows I hate driving, but I had so many children with so many activities that I needed a car. I gave my phone number to a couple of the car dealership, because some of them were not working on a Sunday. I asked God to help me find a car. I said whoever calls me before 8 am will get my business. The guy who sold me the car called me at 7:58 am. He got my sale. This was a big feat. I never liked to drive, but I bought the car to get the children to and fro, to church. The car had issues but it ran well and even drove through heavy snowstorms. The windows would open and close when I bought it, but after a while, you could open the windows but they wouldn't roll back up. I had to hot wire the windows shut. I would take a wire and put one side on the battery and I would tap the window switch with the other side and wahlah…the window would close. One day, this guy called himself trying to help me, but quickly discovered I didn't need his help. He called me MacGyver from the tv show of the guy who could fix anything, lol. I had to put air in the tires monthly. The car was so hot in the summer time, it was a hot box. One day, I hit a pot hole and broke the carriage under the car. It might as well have costed me a million bucks. I loved my car.

The Change

In 2007 several changes happened. I went into early menopause…no more period; my body started aching. I cut my locks off. I lost my voice due to overuse. I attempted to pursue workers compensation but they did not know how to handle the case, so they closed it. I was being constantly checked on by the agency hierarchy. I had nodes on either side of my vocal cords. I changed jobs from working in one Unit answering 100 calls per day to another Unit where I paid health insurance premiums on a reasonable accommodation.

In January of 2007 we sang 6 services at Jubilee Christian Church;3 in the morning and 3 at night as it was Watch Night Service. We wore choir robes.

We were singing *I will bless the Lord.* I sweated so much that my long locks were so heavy that I thought I was going to have whiplash. I decided to cut my locks. I was telling everyone that I was going to cut them but no one believed me.

My menstruation cycle came in January and February but it did not come in March and all of a sudden, my back was so sore, I made a trip to my doctor. She asked if there was a chance that I could be pregnant and my response was," not unless I was Mary, the mother of Jesus." I have been celibate since 2001. She sent me for an MRI and blood test. She called me a couple of weeks later with the results. She said," Leslie you have a little arthritis in your back and then said rapidly, by the way you are in menopause…"at a very early age

The funny part is that I prayed to God and asked when I get married again, was I going to have any more children. I already have 5 children. I guess the answer is, no. I think I have made a fine contribution to society. Don't you?

I looked everywhere to find out who could cut off my locks. I went to my daughter's hair dresser who cut them off, but not before she asked me if I was bleeping crazy. I told her that *I was crazy,* now cut them. She gave me a nice short natural cut. When I drove home (I had a car back), I was sitting in my driveway when I noticed my children in the doorway just staring at me. They did not say a word. They never saw me without locks. I got the locks in 2000 when my youngest was 3 months old. My daughter's aunt locked my hair a month after I divorced their father.

The next day I had a funeral to sing at and rehearsal for Sunday service to go to. I went to sing at the funeral and left. The woman didn't even know it was me. She thought I sent a replacement. When I entered the sanctuary for rehearsal, which was already underway, everyone stopped what they were doing and stared at me as I walked in…in shock. I suppose…I could not believe that no one believed that I was going to cut my locks. I had to. It was time for a change.

I was singing a whole lot that year and answering too many phone calls at work. Every time someone left, they didn't get replaced. I was being overworked. I lost my voice before every now and again due to asthma and then my voice would come back, but this time my voice did not come back. I went to Brigham and Women's hospital and they told me I need surgery. I asked will I be able to sing again after the surgery. Though I could not speak I could still sing. They gave me a speech therapist who said that she would help me learn how to speak again. I asked them the questions once more, "Will I be able to sing again." I told them that I do not care if I ever talk again. They eluded my question. I walked out and told them that I would get a second opinion. I would have respected them more if they just said I don't know.

I just wanted to continue to minister in song, ushering people into God's presence and because singing comforted me in hardest times, when I thought I would not make it to the other side of the trials. Was that so much to ask? No voice, I could not do the job I was doing which consisted of answering 100 calls a day. I did pray to God at the time to get out of that position because it was too taxing on me.

God does answer prayers...

After I was removed from that job, they outsourced the calls to the telephone information center. How do you like them apples? I answered calls for the whole agency single handedly and they sent the calls to a whole information center as my replacement. They gave me a filing project to do temporarily. While I was filing at work next to my colleague who called me Mother Earth, she told me about the voice center which was right across the street from our job.

She told me that is where Julie Andrews went amongst others. At lunch I went straight there. They gave me an appointment for the next day. They took x-rays. They told me that I did need surgery. They explained to me that they would make sure that I could sing again and perhaps even better that I did before. They showed me the x-ray in color. They explained to me in detail their plan to get my voice back especially my singing voice. They were going to fix my vocal cords.

My surgery was set. The voice therapist took me into the studio and asked me to sing. She gave me different tones to emulate and I did. Then I went in for the surgery. The nurse asked me was I scared because I was too calm. I told him that I already prayed and God said he would not take away my worship so I just laid down assuredly and said," I am ready, do your thing." All I heard was 5,4,3…. off to sleep I went. The surgery was a success. I was ordered not to speak for two weeks to allow my throat to heal. That was an interesting time. I had 5 kids. How was that going to work? I think only once did I say something during the two weeks because one of my kids made me angry.

I am not going to mention the child's name but he is my only boy…and it didn't harm anything. Thank God! I walked around doing my version of sign language to communicate with everyone. I also carried around a notebook. I went back to the voice therapist and back into the studio and was told to sing again. I couldn't believe the sound that was coming out of my mouth. Pre-surgery I sang alto for 30 years and could barely hit the high notes. She told me to drink plenty of water an hour prior to singing and to practice breathing when I talk. I did not breath properly when I talked. She informed me that I sang correctly but I did not speak correctly which caused the injury and I am a talker. She also advised me to stay away from spicy foods. That wasn't going to be hard.

Things have definitely changed. One day, I went to Jubilee South and no soprano showed up. So, I got up there and sang soprano. It was flowing out of my mouth. I just let God use me that day. I was a little surprised at the high tones that were flowing from my mouth. Pre-Surgery I could barely hit a middle C...lol. I even got yelled at by the worship leader of the day. He asked me if I was straining. I said no that is what was coming out. He knew that I sang alto for years and that day soprano was flowing out. Until the day he died, he said I was an alto. No Brendan, I am any part you want me to sing. Rest.

Yearly church would audition people to be on the worship team. I was auditioned by Pastor Avril, she was shocked that my voice got so high. She was used to me singing alto as well. I had to learn the soprano parts as I would naturally flow into the alto part which was a little uncomfortable at the time. A lot of changes occurred that year for the better. I was getting ready for what was to come. I was about to do bigger and better things.

My second grand was born during my no voice ordeal. They named her Audrey. She likes to be called Dee. She is smart beautiful and very flexible. She used to get up without using her hands. When she was 1 and her brother was three, they had a full toddler discussion as to whether they should call me grandma or call me Yaya, like I asked them to call me. For a spell they were calling me grandma. They both agreed that they should just call me Yaya since that is what I asked to be called. When she asked for something to drink, she referred to me as Yaya. At that point, I was ready to give her anything that she asked for and more.

One day I was visiting with them and was watching a robot cartoon. Her sister called the robot fat. She said," I don't know why you called the robot fat, when you don't call Yaya fat." Did she just call me fat? She sure did. Ever since she was young, her conversation was that of an old soul just like her mother. The apple doesn't fall far from the tree, huh?

Unwelcomed Spirit

After all the changes of 2007 there were trials and tribulations coming my way left and right.

Anxiety and depression are trying to invade my family. Stand firm and the devil shall flee from you. First this spirit was in my ex-husband and I thought it had gone. There is a spirit who keeps showing up in my daughter, Tyra. It is called disobedience and disrespect. It actually jumped into all of my children. I think it jumped into them since my ex-husband is now gone. I used to think that it was something that I was doing wrong, but then I was reminded that trials will come but I had the victory through Jesus Christ. There must be a spiritual door that is open that the unwelcomed spirit keeps entering. I am going to find that door and shut it.

It would try to tell me what I should and should not do and then say it's not talking to me, as if it is ok to disrespect me. It was snapping at me telling me when it was doing things and telling me that I am just going to have to wait, as if it was the parent and not me? Tyra had been running away since she was 13 years old. The situation had me questioning, *am I a bad mom,* yet again. I realize I do too much for these kids and they take advantage. There was a time when Tyra blatantly left the house after I asked her not to. She thought she was going to be able to disrespect me, not tell me where she was going, be gone all day, and then come back home. I told her that if she was not going to listen to my instruction or discipline, that she could not come back home. So, she did not come back home. I was told to file a missing-persons report, but I did not. I am always saving the children from themselves. This time, I would see how long this would play out. She was about to start school. I wondered who was going to buy her school supplies or school clothes. I could tell you who was not running out and doing that. She was with that boy. She didn't understand that she couldn't take care of herself with no money. If she wanted to run someone's house that is what she was going to have to do, get her own apartment. Tyra was gone for a time. Though I missed her, I did not miss the disrespect. When you don't know what to do, you should stand still and that is exactly what I did. I was trying to find out how I should respond to her when she did come around because I knew she would eventually come around.

I finally asked Tyra to come home where she is supposed to be. I had to figure out how to deal with her when she was being disrespectful and disobedient. She came back. Tyra got mad because I was unable to turn on her phone when she wanted it turned on, and she left yet again. I was so concerned for my daughter …she has attitude outbursts. She gets sick when we travel. We discovered it was anxiety. Lately though, it has been getting worse as she gets older. She becomes destructive. What am I to do? I would take her to the doctors. She was referred to mental health and was given a college student as a counselor. She also had a counselor who came to our house but because we didn't qualify for Mass Health those services were terminated. She had nothing and left. It is terrible being middle classed. You make too much money to receive aid and too little to afford the best care. Then she was assigned a counselor at BMC. She visited this counselor for over a year and the behavior did not change. At her physical appointment, they referred her to neurology for her headaches where they determined that they were being caused by her anxiety and the fact that she wasn't eating or drinking enough.

In Philadelphia, while I was at Keala's school for open house, she had me in the hospital for dehydration. It was a little scary because they said that she was not good. After 4 bags of fluid, we left the out of state hospital and took the bus back home to Massachusetts. I must have explained her symptoms a million times to the mental health faculty but she was never diagnosed with anything. Every school that she attended was concerned, but thought that it was just her and she could control it. I believe she can control it sometimes, but then I also think that sometimes she has an episode and that she can't reel it back in so easily. The child is extremely bright and genuinely a good person until that anger episode get a hold of her. Then, I want to beat it out of her. Whether I was quiet or said something, the girl would get mad and say she needs to go for a walk; even at night when it was too late for her to be out. When will she finally get the help she needs, it is exhausting that I think of it, her father did that. He would go from 0 to 10 in a minute. One minute he was happy, the next minute he didn't want to be around anyone. He would then just tuck himself in the room; even if we have a house full of people. Maybe he was never diagnosed and resorted to drugs. I will not claim this for my child. I am going to love it out of her. She is victorious. She belongs to God.

The other children have some form of anxiety also. Alicia was taking Ubers back and forth to work. She would freak out on public transportation. Keala gets overwhelmed quickly. One time she had us in the hospital and she was told that she had an anxiety episode. I am sure the others must have felt that I did not love them, as much time as I spent trying to get help for Tyra. I don't really know about Norman because he grew up in the gym. I do know he always had to have someone with him when he went for jobs or school or even to be on a time. Maybe that is a form of anxiety as well. And come to think of it, Tiana has a little also. When she is going through, you will not hear from her. You can call or text her and get her voicemail. Don't wait for a return phone call. Your hair will turn gray. This child has been holding me for some unforetold reason and she gets belligerent.

I started praying and rebuking and then I started singing praising God, seeking God's face … I pray without ceasing that this unwelcomed spirit has to leave my child/children. They are children of the Most-High.

For we wrestle not against flesh and blood but against principalities, against powers, against the rulers of darkness of this world, against spiritual wickedness in high places. Ephesians 6:12

God did not give us a spirit of fear; but he has given unto power, love, and a sound mind. I pray to God for clarity on how to handle the situation in the physical, while God works out the situation behind the scenes.

You see that unwelcomed spirit can't stay where God is. It has to leave. God lives in this home. I will worship harder to keep spirits that want to keep jumping off out and powerless like it really is…

When I was growing up, I didn't think my parents knew what was good for me. Yet now, I look back and realize that they did have a clue and that they were trying to protect me from dangers and heartbreak. One day my children will see that I am and was only wanting them to become the best they could be. I sing "you can't have my family, you can't have my increase, you can't have my breakthrough. I plead the blood of Jesus"

There is always something trying to block your blessings. Generational curses are real. My eldest started having babies in her teens just like I did. She had 4 children with her husband, just like I did. I used to ask her why she was following my footsteps. I used to tell her to make her own. We both work for the government. We are both divorced. We are both single parents. I hope that she finds out her worth faster than I did. I had to learn who I was while mothering 4 more children. That is no easy feat. Good thing we both are worshippers and we both have God.

My last child went to several schools as well. She went to 2 different middle schools and 4 different high schools in 4 years. Does that sound familiar? She changed schools due to explosive anxiety episodes. The schools tried to accommodate her, but decided they could no longer. She went to an alternative school which gave her college credits.

She attended her first year of college as a sophomore. She was also supposed to be going to Quinsigamond Community College, but ended up at Rugby Community College, my alma mater. She lived with her boyfriend. I lived with mine at that time. For a minute, I freaked out about it because I did not want her to follow my footsteps either. I gave her and that situation to God. Therefore, though we have been through troubles, we win.

This Scripture Comes To Mind

This day I call the heavens and the earth as witnesses against you that I have set before you, life and death, blessings and curses. Now choose life, so that you and your children may live 20 and that you may love the Lord your God, listen to his voice, and hold fast to him. For the Lord is your life, and he will give you many years in the land he swore to give to your fathers, Abraham, Isaac and Jacob.

Deuteronomy 30:19-20

I want them to know they have a choice like the scripture says. The choices that they make will determine their destiny. Generational curses and chains are broken. Singing the Song break every chain, and believe that it is so.

In 2010, I got rid of the best car I ever had. It was time for inspection to get a new sticker. The law had just changed. It said that if a light is on in your car you cannot get a sticker. The part that I needed was going to cost me $500 just for the piece and $250 for labor. It was either pay to repair car, or feed the children. Children I picked you. I donated the car to cars for causes. I have driven people's car but to date I have yet to purchase another car. I went back to public transportation.

In the same year, my 3rd grand was born. Her name is Karen. This one is so smart beautiful and swift. When she was 2, we were talking about fire because she was trying to touch the fire extinguisher. I told her that she couldn't touch that and I said fire can be bad, but could she tell me what good fire is used for. She said, "to say happy birthday, to cook her food." I was surprised by her answer, being she was so young. She had a paper plate which she ripped in half. She said," Look Yaya, I have two moons." Then she ripped the moon in half and asked if I wanted a slice of pizza. The toddler knew geometry before she was 3. One day she was fighting with her sister and threw her shoe at her. Her sister told her mother that she hit her.

My daughter said," Both of you keep your hands to yourselves" and Karen said, "I did." She threw a shoe. She did not use her hand. She and her brother called me. I told him that I have his gift and asked her what she'd like for her birthday. She told me that I am always buying for them and then asked me what do I like. I didn't know what to tell her, because no one ever asked me that question before. I had to think about it. I then told her what I liked and she told me to remind her when my birthday comes back around. The child has such a giving heart.

In 2011, I was on my way to rehearsal. I stepped off of the bus at train station. There was an indentation in the brick sidewalk. My foot twisted on the indentation and while it was twisted my body landed on it. A group of people who were on the bus with me, picked me up and put me on the bench. The bus inspector came over and took my statement about what happened and then called the ambulance. The bus that I stepped off of didn't even check on me to see if I was okay before pulling off. The ambulance ride was bumpy and painful. I got to the emergency room and they had me on a gurney in the hallway for a long while. They sent me home with an air cast. My ankle was swollen like a balloon. This ankle had me back and forth to the hospital for pain. I have several ankle braces. I went to their physical therapist and I even had a cortisone shot.

The ankle did not break, but I tore all of the ligaments and cartilage in the ankle. I pray that one day my ankle will be totally healed. Periodically, the ankle throbs and I have to walk gingerly on it, because it feels like it doesn't want to hold this beautiful body up.

In 2012, my last grand but certainly not least was born. Ira is what they named him and he is so fun. He dances like nobody's business. I told him that I liked his jacket. He said," It's not a jacket. I asked" Then what is it? He replied" It is not a jacket." Then I said," I like your blazer." He replied," Yesssss, thank you!" The boy knows the difference between a blazer and a jacket at a young age. He loves cars. His conversation, like his siblings, is very advanced as well. He and his sister Karen were talking about fake Santa. They were trying to convince me that Santa was black and every other Santa was fake. The Uber driver, whose car we were in during the conversation, was thoroughly entertained. He is a testament to his name which means laughter.

From Jubilee Christian Church to Fellowship Christian Church

I heard from God in 2013 to leave Jubilee, so I began visiting other churches. I was still singing in the choir. In fact, I was asked to sing whatever part they lacked. There was a Sunday that I sang all three parts; in the morning service I sang soprano, because no soprano showed up, I sang alto at the second service and tenor at the third. I was used to being at everyone's disposal so I just agreed to sing whenever they asked.

I visited every church from Grace Church to Kingdom Builders. While I was visiting, I did not hear God tell me to move to any of the ones I visited. Signs that I needed to leave kept presenting themselves throughout the year. Things were changing at the church, and it was evident that I was old news. I attended Jubilee when it was New Covenant Christian center, for 23 years. Perhaps because Mel and my cousin were going through a divorce, they took it out on me. I am not sure, but signs were pointing to the door. One day, I was at rehearsal at Jubilee and the worship leader of the hour came in and did a half prayer, then she told everyone to get on stage.... God was not invited to that rehearsal. I did not sing on that Sunday because I felt that God was not represented there. I needed worship this day as my uncle passed away that particular year. Worship was absent.

After this incident, a guest worship leader was invited to lead worship. She started to rehearse and stopped the rehearsal. She asked Pastor Avril if she could say something. Pastor Avril gave her the okay. She told everyone who had unforgiveness in their heart to go forgive whomever they were holding and come back with a clean heart. She told everyone who was sleeping with or living with their boyfriend to go sit down. She told them that is all about Jesus and not about us. I told Pastor Avril this information months earlier.

I spoke with Shane Chocolate one night about the situation and he said something very interesting. He said why did it take an outsider to tell them that God was not represented in worship, when you told them months prior? It puts a question on whether they respected me enough to listen to me. Wow! This was an eye opener. The last sign happened on New Year's Eve. The choir I was on sang, and then Pastor Avril had a special worship team that I wasn't a part of. I prayed the New year in and asking the lord and praying that I want to do what HE says do and I want to go where HE wanted me to go.

The special worship team got up and started singing Moving Forward. That was my last day at Jubilee Christian church.

That was on a Wednesday. While I was praying, I asked God where to go. He asked who do I pray with. I answered Dora and Carina. He said, what church do they go to and I answered Fellowship Christian church. That Sunday, me and my kids attended Fellowship Christian Church. Keala turned to me and said I belong to that church. I now belong to Fellowship Christian Church. I became a worship leader. I had to pick songs, teach them, and lead them on

Sunday. I did it while the Lead Worship leader was out of town. I had to step up.

At the end of February, after I left Jubilee, I received a call from Pastor Avril's assistant asking me to sing alto. I was gone for 8 weeks. I hadn't been to Thursday rehearsals and I was one of the consistent goers. I explained that the reason that I did not formally leave is because I had to wait to speak with Pastor Copper, who I was accountable to. Pastor Copper called me yearly asking how everybody was and then bidding you good bye.... It was usually a 5-minute check in.

She said that she would relay the message to Pastor Avril. I got a hold of Pastor Copper who was about to preach at Fellowship, the intended church. He was in Ephesians 4:18 when I called. I told him that I was leaving Jubilee and joining Fellowship Christian Church. I explained to him that I not only sang, I wrote poetry and songs, but I was never able to utilize any other talent at Jubilee as they had their own favorites.

Pastor Copper said that Ephesians 4 said that the church was supposed to help you use your gifts to the glory of God. He then gave the ok to leave. I called Pastor Avril's assistant back and asked her how to formally leave the church. She said that I should send an email and cc everyone. I wrote a nice email thanking them for introducing me to Christ and teaching me about the Lord. That is how I came to serve at Fellowship Christian Church. I know this is where

I am supposed to be. God called me to this church, so that people attached to me would come to church and get to know God more.

Trials And Tribulations Then Blessings

There was a time when I only had 60 cents in my pocket. I told my colleague, Brenda, that I was not worried because God also takes care of me. I received a call from the lobby. It was my ex-husband, who was my husband at the time. We were separated, but he came to my job and gave me 60 dollars. I then had $60.60. God is awesome!

One day, on a Friday, I paid all my bills and was left with 10 dollars. I wasn't going to be paid until the next Friday. I prayed and asked the Lord to send help. I didn't even have money to pay for food for the children. I went outside and the neighbor Shane asked me if I needed a ride to the bus stop. I agreed. He told me not to leave. He went into the post office then into the bank.

He came back out and gave me two hundred dollars. I was taken aback. I cried all the way to work. God answered my prayer instantaneously. I called Shane when I got to work and explained that I only had 10 dollars in my pocket when he blessed me. He said he was glad that God used him .

At work they had a mass downsizing. I still work there, though I got a one-day suspension wrongfully and I was commended the next day for calling emergency when one of my colleagues fell ill. I was looking to see how much I was going to get on my next check. I calculated a low figure, subtracting the one day's pay. When I looked at the pay stub, it was higher than I had calculated. Then I found out that I got a raise. My God is an awesome God. He knew that I still needed money to pay bills and the raise came at a great time…coincidence or not. I think not. God takes care of you. What the devil meant for evil, God turned around for good.

Though my telephone and my keyboard at work were antiquated, I received a new telephone cord and a new keyboard. I usually would have to wait weeks for them to fix anything at work.

My Word 2016 subscription expired and they wanted me to re subscribe for $100 for one year. I felt that was too much money. My brother gave me a website. I bought word 2019 for 60 dollars.

One morning I woke up late to the point where I would have had to run for the train. Just as I started to run, one of my fellow train riders drove by and scooped me up. She had a green Volvo wagon like I used to have. It was dejavu. We got to the train platform and someone mentioned that it was May. I forgot my lunch and my May bus pass at home. I was going to go back home and make lunch, get bus pass, and get on at a later train. Just then, a stranger said, don't do that. He handed me a twenty-dollar bill and told me I can pay him back when I can. I was beside myself. God's favor was definitely upon me.

When I got to work one day, the workers were painting fences outside and the fumes came into my office through the vents causing me to have to run out before my throat closed. I ended up having a free day, because they sent me to a training room upstairs from my office. Since I didn't have all applications on the computer to do my job, I was basically relaxing.

For lunch, I didn't have to spend money because my colleague had a head of lettuce, salad dressing croutons and tuna. We had tuna salad for 2 days.

I got a letter in the mail that said my second mortgage is eligible for forgiveness...I almost fell out of my chair. I even called the place to find out if it was a hoax. It was not. The City of Boston has its perks. I am so elated. My finances have been funky and now this blessing came with $20,000 being forgiven. It ended up being a nightmare and a blessing at the same time, because, it turns out I was misinformed by the City of Boston employee about what part of the mortgage was forgiven. I found out that only four thousand dollars, which was closing costs, was forgiven and that I should have continued paying my second mortgage. Even though I explained that I was misinformed, the bank did not excuse my late payments and I was unable to get the refinancing that year.

Jehovah Jireh...so I had been trying to refinance my home and withdraw money, because I wanted to pay off my debt and only have my bills to pay, but it hadn't come through yet. My son needs to pay his tuition and housing and I was calling on the name of Jesus for God to supply what we needed. Though I did not get the refinancing at that time, God still provided funds for Norman to attend school.

I co-signed for two of my children's student loans. The monthly payment was an ungodly amount which I could not afford. God allowed me to get the refinancing a year after the denial of the first refinance application; perhaps because he knew I was going to have to pay kid's student loans and the refinancing made it possible. I also believe that the Lord stopped the refinancing application because a year later I was approved for a refinancing with a different bank at a lower rate.

One day, I was walking to the train and I found twenty-dollar bill on an empty cigarette box. The next day, I was walking down the street again and found another twenty-dollar bill. Forty dollars found in two days. Woot-woot! I still need to learn how to be much wiser in my financial decisions. I should never have co-signed for kid's student loans. Now, I have to pay the price.

Do not be one of those who shakes hands in a pledge one of those who surety (co-sign) for debt. How could I have missed this scripture...

Proverbs 22:26

I didn't think I was going to make it to my next paycheck due to so many unexpected expenses...i.e., my daughter went to Baltimore and I had to pay for baggage. It was a little itty-bitty bag and it costed fifty-two dollars. Then, I went to the dentist and had to pay a co-pay of fifty-five dollars that I had to look for. Later, I had to pay for my baby to come back from Baltimore which cost sixty-two dollars. I was also sending money to my daughter in Philly until her first paycheck. I explained to her, it was time to be responsible, no more buying clothes "You have too many articles of clothing and you only have one body. You are now going to be responsible for self and will have to learn how to pay for things such as food, shelter, and clothing while in school. Of course, I will help, but it is time to grow up." I am proud of that one though, because she is striving to be a better her... Despite all the expenses, I made it!

There was a week where I was sick and there were so many things happening, including my baby breaking her hand and only one person showing up to rehearsal for Sunday's service. Then, that one person was trying to bail out. God fixed everything. I was healed. They tended to my baby with my permission over the phone, and God sent two more choir members to serve that Sunday. I know that God was with me, because I would have never been able to get through that week in my own Strength.

What an experience I had in Boston Bowl! I paid and went to the lane they gave me. Then, a white family came and said they had the lane I had. They went and got someone who came and asked me for my receipt, almost accusing me of stealing the lane. It turned out that their system gave two lane 28s.The person moved us to lane 30...while we were first. I didn't argue. We just moved to lane 30. We put our things on lane 31s table, but that was because it was closed to lane 30. Then that same person came and said if someone comes for lane 31 that we would have to move our stuff again. What was that person's problem? We were only there to have fun because Norman was going back to college the next morning. It bothered me so much that I called on Monday morning. I spoke with customer service. She asked me to describe the man. I did. She thought it might've been a cleaning person, but said there were no cleaning people that met that description. She then transferred me to the general manager. I soon discovered that it was the general manager who lacked customer service and diversity skills. He didn't even apologize. He said that I misconstrued what happened. I perceived the situation incorrectly. He thought that I was uneducated and didn't understand the words that were coming out of his mouth; maybe because I was black.

I called the owners. I spoke with a Jerry Mils. He apologized for the treatment I received. He also sent me a package for free bowling but I thanked him for the free stuff and told him I would be happier if they got the general manager to take diversity and customer service training.

Another instance of how good God is was when last year I took the Megabus and missed my connecting bus due to traffic. While I was on the bus, I called their Customer service and was led to believe that I would get a refund or at least a pass onto another bus and to call them back if I missed the connecting bus. They came back on the line and said that they were not going to refund my money, because I should have had two hours between the two buses...nowhere on their website did I find that. Anyway, they made me buy another ticket to get on the next bus and did not send it to my email. Their office closed and the guy had to go through hoops to find my reservation that they just made. He found the reservation and I got home... Fast forward, we were supposed to get on a 10:55 pm bus. It left at 1 am. I received

50% off of that trip which was more money that they ne-glected to refund me the year before. The moral of the story is that the person(s) who wrong you will have to pay you back one way or another. It will come back to you. You need not worry...sing!

Someone used my information and applied for Virid-ian Energy without my consent. I got in contact with the con-sumer relations who was telling me that they couldn't do an-ything. You mean told tell me that someone can use my in-formation and I am not protected? I called the city councilors office and I haven't heard from them yet. I called the attor-ney general's office who told me to call the Federal Trade Commission. They filed an identity theft report on my behalf and I have to go on and finish it. I was also instructed to file a police report against the person and contact my creditors. My finances are definitely being attacked. I was put in touch with the Department of Public Utilities, who resolved the problem and paid me whatever was erroneously charged to me. Since this incident, my bills have been lower than they have ever been. Before the cold weather hit, my gas bill was 15 dollars.

I have been trying to save money, so I have been making my lunch. One day, I didn't have time to make lunch. I was about to go out and buy lunch. Just as I was walking out, a colleague came down and said that one of our col-leagues is leaving the agency and they are having a farewell party for her. Go up and bid her good bye and there is plenty of food. What? I didn't have to spend money.

I always get signs. I went to Pastor Angie's women's ministry. I was asked by Lola and then by Carina. I could not say no. I have been talking to God about my financial problems. I am so in the hole that I cannot see my way out. But I asked God to help me. We were talking about Who's your daddy. God and Papi …Love my daddies. They are there to protect provide love and encourage.

After women's group, Ma Mirna gave me $162 towards the $1,000 dollars that I asked for from God. God really does work things out for your good. Then, Donna called and said that she would also help me. I just wanted to get up and do a praise dance. God also gave me great parents who care about my welfare. I love and cherish them so much. They helped their children, grandchildren, and great-grands, which is a blessing that they are able to do that. I am now able to see the legacy that I will leave behind for my children and grands for generations yet to come… I am not going to be afraid of trying new things and exploring better options. I woke up so downcast one morning, I immediately started worshipping God in song. It lifted my spirit as I walked down the street to my train. I was praying that God answer me about if my walk with Him was pleasing to him. I got on the train and was talking with my train buddies when one of them gifted me with two bracelets. I did not expect it, but I knew in my heart that it was from God.

I went to my friend's house to buy a leather ring that she made. We had conversations and were experiencing the same things. I asked her how much was a purse that was hanging in her work room. She gifted it to me. I was speechless…then I went to breakfast, which was delightful. Following, I went to get a manicure from my friend. After I left my friend, I got to the train station and I saw the bus that goes to

Brockton. I was about to jump on it and take a visit to my brother's house. I then decided not to, because I was tired and it was getting kind of late. I went downstairs to the train and I met my brother's friend from 6 grade.

We had a great conversation about life and life choices that we made good and bad. He said that he knows who holds his tomorrow and that Jesus is his Lord and savior. He is not afraid to tell anyone. I discovered that he is discerning like I am. I encouraged him to read about Daniel and Joseph in the Bible. He claims that he knows when people are sick or when they are not going to live. I said, sometimes that's would makes you feel different. He said that he wanted to buy a house. He said that I bought my house years ago. I explained that if it is Gods will, the house could cost a million bucks and you could still get it. What was crazy was that he was going to the same area I was going to. His barbershop was at the end of my street. That was God setting me up to minister to him. He didn't have a church home, so I invited him to mine. Since then, he's attended my church several times.

I went to the post office to mail a package. I didn't have tape, which is usually provided by them, so I went down the street to Walgreens and asked if they sold packaging tape. I was told no. One of the ladies went back and got packaging tape. She came back and taped my package up for me. She did not have to do that. That, was very nice of her. I went and shipped the package.

Accompanied by trumpets cymbals and other instruments, the singers raise their voices in praise to the Lord and say He is good and His mercies endureth forever, and the temple was filled with a cloud. My life is proof of how good God is and how He blesses me and keeps me each and every day...

2nd Chronicles 5:13, 14

One Sunday, I was out of town so I decided to watch the service on Facebook live. Pastor Donald was talking about peace. I had the TV on simultaneously with the radio, but it was on mute. All of a sudden Pastor Donald started talking about we have angels to protect us. As he mentioned angels, the movie Heaven is for Real showed the part when the boy walked into the church which turned into the sky and angels were flying around. I believe they were my angels camped about me. Hallelujah...God is truly amazing.

This is the first year in my life that I owe the feds money in the thousands. The bank I had my mortgage with was acquired by another bank and didn't report it to the credit bureau, so it dropped my credit score. Yet God saw fit to have someone from church gift me a car. I walked in church and she said," Leslie, I need to talk to you." She asked if I needed a car. I told her that I didn't have any money. She said that she is gifting me her car. I asked," C-A-R." She said" yes." I am now the new owner of a car.

116

Work Shenanigans

Things were very interesting at work. I would be working like crazy at my desk, and then when I got ready to go to lunch, I would see my colleague and two bosses having a meeting, without me. I know God always sets me apart. He told me not to worry about them and that he has me.

My whole entire work life I was always left to work on my own. I was given permission performing managerial tasks without the title. Work has been so crazy to the point where I'd look up and it was lunchtime, and then I'd look up again and then it was time to go home. I am there because my testimony and light are needed there. I am an investigator…my brain is built to investigate. I was nosey, so I guess that is a skill that works for this field of work. I also like to dot my I's and cross my T's…I have been accused of being too thorough. I had my evaluation at work. The boss said that my investigations are extremely thorough causing me to lack time management…lol. I asked if I am being reprimanded for accuracy. She said no. Then, she mentioned my time management again.

I have 3 workflows, 20 cases in my drawer, and at the mercy of the bosses, and other outside offices. Not to mention, I answer 2 phone lines.

There are only 7.5 hours in a day and I don't recall have a big "S" on my chest suggesting I am superwoman. I felt like singing that song that Karyn White wrote a long time ago, *I'm not your superwoman.*

One day, I got suspended from work for one day without pay after 30 year. They said that I was using the computer to seek out family information…me? I am investigator. I investigate…I am also very popular and I am going to run into people's claims, including family, but I will not misuse information. I can't even steal a piece of candy good. Also, I had asthma episodes and had to use Albuterol and sometimes Prednisone, which would cause me my mind to wander more than usual. I felt very devalued at work. I did. Work seems to been being piled on me. I just worked the best to my ability. The day after I came back from serving suspension I was commended for a "heroic act."

It was hard for me to do all the paperwork they want done. I hope they remember that I am human and not a machine or computer. I have a suspicion that I was being tested to go to another level; just like God moved me from Jubilee to Fellowship. It came to the point where I felt like I was being pushed out. I am working so hard I find myself in bed by 8 and sleeping by 9. Sometimes, I even have a headache and don't even want to look at my phone at all after work.

I have been yelled at by hierarchy several times. I was accused of being on a personal call. It was a manager in another department. Not sure why they felt the need to do so. But it was uncalled for.

We had a meeting. I explain I am a worker. I come to work to work. I don't hear anything when being yelled at. Apologies were rendered.

It reminded me of a former boss I had who did the same thing. She accused me of coming back late from my lunch, when I went to lunch late because I was covering phones while she was in a meeting.

My whole entire work life I have always been misunderstood. Looking back, I only had a small few bosses who understood me and allow me to flow.

A colleague of mine came and gave me paperwork, then he said that he had done my work before and that I am not irreplaceable. I asked what he was saying and he went on to say that people think that they are irreplaceable. I just thanked him for the paperwork and told him to have a nice day.

Another colleague doesn't even talk to me because he asked me about work on my lunch. I told him that I was on my lunch and he said, "It would only take one-minute Christ, Leslie." I told him that we were not going there. He will not be demanding anything from me. I told him that he is not my boss and even my boss will not talk to me that way. He now says absolutely nothing to me. People are really thinking they can talk to people any type of way. I think not. One day, I sneezed and he blessed me because he thought the sneeze came from my colleague… That was hilarious. I pray that he finds peace. I did nothing to the man except not tolerated his disrespectfulness.

I do so much work at my job that the field thinks I am the manager. I am constantly invited to manager's meetings, yet I am not a manager. I believe I am still there because God is still using me there.

I have one colleague that actually defended me to the bosses. He told the bosses that I am the one who does all the work and my colleague doesn't do enough and they don't appreciate me... I couldn't believe he said that to them. He is usually a quiet one. He looks out for me. When I am working passed my lunch time, he reminds me to go to lunch. I have conversations with him. He is very knowledgeable about life, financial resources, organizational skills and a little sense of humor. People don't know that about him, because he doesn't speak much to anyone. I appreciate him. All other colleagues except the one who doesn't speak to me are fairly close, and we actually check on each other outside of work especially my colleague I go to lunch with who has to be a guinea pig to test my jokes on her. She reminds me of my childhood friend Marissa.

Though busy, the climate of the job has been better. The problem might have been that what I see as a completed case is not what another might consider a completed case. Since I am the investigator, one would think I have the right to make the decision that I make, and it doesn't make my decisions incorrect. People call me, email me, or come to my desk for everything. .

It is still incredibly busy at work. My boss has been giving me case after case after case, but she came to my desk and said that she really appreciates me because she realizes that she has been piling work on me and I am the best. When she said that to me, I asked if I am being fired? She laughed and said no. That was the first time that she actually acknowledged my work ethic to me. .

Some chains are being broken.

I wonder…is it the color of my skin? I give it to God. As I pray for those I work with and for, I continue to pray that I am humble and not making decisions in my emotions. I also want to make sure that I am honoring those who are in authority, my boss.

Work willingly at whatever you do, as though you were working for the Lord rather than for other people.

Colossians 3:23

Don't Be Scurd

I fear driving on the highway but I did it anyhow. I feared heights, I still get on the elevator to high level floors. I even have stage fright from time to time to the point that I would forget the words of a song. Fear can keep you from accessing your full potential...tell it bye.

The Bible says don't be scared and do not be afraid several times; probably because life can be scary. We fear what we do not understand or the unknown. Here is something to ponder. Why is it we are not scared to do bad things? That's why you see fights on Facebook, as well as bullying, racism and the like. But yet when it comes to pursing your God given purpose, we are scared to take a step.

As I said at the beginning of this book fear probably delayed the writing of this book. Fear has taken up too much of my life. God did not give us the spirit of fear. He gave us the spirit of power, love, and a sound mind. Though I read this scripture, I didn't believe it until now. Fear no longer makes decisions for me. 50th year....I just now came to a realization that when it came to business and my finances I would shun away from it. I didn't want to join business ventures and was even afraid to refinance the house. I have been paying a high rate for years. I now realize that sometimes you just need to jump in the water and have faith. God has taken good care of me thus far, but I believe my finances could have been better a long time ago. I believe I put that fear into my children. I must now show by example, not to be afraid of paperwork regarding business and finances. I must learn how to invest and how to save and not live pay check to pay check.

That is not the way to live. I have been doing it for the past 50 years. If I didn't have God, I would have probably been homeless by now. I don't want this for my children. I want my children to fly high …no limits… I did tell them how to buy food to make inexpensive meals. I explained that you can't go crazy buying things that you don't need. Grown folks cannot come back and live off of mama. Here I am telling about saving money and how to handle money, yet I don't even know how my mortgage was calculated. I should have known better than to co-sign for the kids' college. I gave Norman the benefit of the doubt that he was going to finish college but he barely made it through high school. I guess God had to get my attention using drastic measures. Today, I can say I will longer let fear dictate my decisions. I will trust God.

I read in the Bible that the disciples were complaining that they had to pay taxes. Jesus told them to go fishing at the Jordan and the first fish that they catch, to open its mouth and take a coin and use it to pay the taxes. If Jesus got a coin from a fish's mouth, I should not be afraid because he can show me where to get the money to pay off my debt. We will be victorious; no fear. Do you have faith? Hebrew 11:1 Now faith is the substance of things hoped for, the evidence of things not seen. You have to have genuine faith. And everyone has faith, because if they didn't they wouldn't sit on a chair or eat out or even walk out the door for fear that something would happen. We can't be scared while we wait either. Fear cancels faith. It is the complete opposite of faith. Believe, Believe, Believe and wait, wait, wait …It will be worth it. I remember when I couldn't wait to be married and now, I am divorced (happily).

I wasn't saved then and I didn't know God like I know Him now. I was serving in church but was not intimate with Him. I was going through the motions… I know that now, because I look at my children. The only ones who were baptized right now is my oldest girl and my last one, who got baptized with the freezing cold waters one year in the month of October. Everyone else, is hanging on the fence. They do know there is a God, but have not surrendered to Him yet. I decided to pray a different way for them and not take it out on them that they are not saved and baptized. I pray and wait. Also, the Bible says that you and your whole household will be saved, Amen. I pray that I go to another level financially…so I can do things for the kingdom and help others. People take it for granted when they say that prayer works, and it does. So that means, everything that you pray for, that is in line with God's will, shall be granted. I believe it is so, so it will be so. If I didn't have faith, I would be locked up in some mental hospital somewhere because of some of the things I have gone through in my life. God is faithful. This is why I sing praise unto Him.

2017 Wonders

Early 2017, I got a scare. They found an abnormality in my mammogram. They had me come back in three weeks and still saw it. They set me up for a biopsy. I got to the biopsy appointment and they decided that they could not perform the biopsy because the issue was too deep in my breast. They decided to give me another mammogram in 6 mos. I went back and they still saw the same issue. I went back in another six months and they still saw it; the issue. I was praying and had people interceding for me. I went back six months later. They looked and looked and looked and the abnormality was gone. It could have been fat, because I had lost about twenty pounds. I was not eating sugar or carbohydrates. I couldn't remember when the last time was that I used the asthma pump. God was working it out behind the scenes. You see why I serve and worship God? He is a good God. I have to tell you I was scared. I know I should not have been because God is with me, but I have to get my teeth out and I am ready but then again, I am not. Since I had blood issues for most of my life, I was chewing everything such as ice or anything that was crunchy, which damaged my teeth.

I've been to several dentists, and for some reason though they say that they can help me with my teeth, they give me the run around, having me use all my sick leave for nothing. I will find the right dentist who will help me smile with confidence again. After all, I am a jokester and need to laugh with a beautiful smile. I know if I have my teeth fixed,

I will be better health wise. That is the only reason I am doing it, because I would like to live a long life.

August 5, 2017

While going through the health scares, I rededicated my life to the Lord by getting baptized again. It was a beautiful day. My siblings, except Renan and Rona came about and my children Alicia and Tyra came to support me. God is truly awesome. Everything about it was different...For example, we moved down from where we typically baptized people. Then, we prayed in a little group as opposed to the whole group who came. Then, when the pastor did the renunciation, we did not hold hands. I went down in the water and came up with a higher expectation. I am changed. God has already spoken to me, and I decided to make some changes in my life. In my whole saved life, I was never prophesied on. I went to different revivals and to services that had Prophets attend and I never ever received a prophesy. They would call the person next to me or the person beside me but it was never me, until August 20, 2017.

I lead worship at church and God came down to dwell among us. I tell you the spirit was thick in the air. After church, I was bidding everyone a great week. I walked outside and there was a lady sitting in her car.... The Lord told me to hug her. She was already in the car, but I immediately walked to the driver seat side and she got out to hug me...Then she said in my ear," Oh that high blood pressure has to go," she said, "finish writing your book", "put money in her pocket a whole heap", "the job that you want you have it you have to go and get it, your husband is coming you just have to keep doing God's will, and my music ministry is bigger than I think and that I should keep worshipping and praising Jesus." I was dumbfounded. I thought the hug was for her, but it was for me. She was all in my closet.

I usually discern for others, but I never had me read like that in my life. She even said I know sometimes you feel like you're by yourself because of your ability but she wants me to know that I am never alone. God walks with me.

My prayer has been answered. There is a song that says Open the eyes of my heart Lord Open the eyes of my heart, I wanna see you, I wanna see you.

That day, I received new eyes. I knew that God loved me enough to send someone to tell me that He loves me and I am on his mind. Ever since then, I knew that I am doing what I am supposed to be doing, SINGING WORSHIP and PRAISES to the Almighty God, and I am hearing music... after song, love songs after love songs to my Lord.

I get a text from this known Pastor. He tells me that God spoke to him about me. He asked if I wanted to be married and I said yes. He said that God has heard my cry. He said that he will pray to ask God who it is ... and let me know. He said that the husband will be good for me and not to be afraid when he reveals himself to me. I told him if he is from God I will know.

He blessed me and I him (September 11, 2017) Back to singing and praising and praying I go.

Dreams

I am a dreamer. I've been dreaming ever since I could remember. Some are clear cut and understandable, and some dreams are complex and come in pieces as if I am putting a puzzle together.

- When I was 15 years-old I had a dream of a baby named Darwin Christof. I thought it was going to be my son but God gave me another name for my son and my son did not look like a Darwin. Fast forward. My daughter had a baby and she named him after his father, you guessed it his name is Darwin. My daughter had another son and you guessed it again.

She named this son Ira but his middle name is Christof. So, when I was 15, I had a dream of my grandsons.

- I had a dream that I was singing on stage an original song. I had on a blue pantsuit with stars all over it, kind of like the night sky. My song hit #1 on the charts. Songs are pouring out of my spirit and I am trying to get them out. We shall see, we shall see if this one will come true. Most dreams I have come true sooner or later.

- I had a dream about a friend of mine. I walked into a church and there was a wedding going on. It was in a church I never saw before, a rather large church, but I couldn't see the parties (the groom or the bride) until he turned around… I saw my friend clearly and although the bride turned also around, I didn't know her…All I knew is she had long brown hair. The church was beautiful and the bride's color was purple. I told my friend about the dream. He kind of answered me as if I was crazy. Fast forward...I attended his wedding in Vermont and his wife had long brown hair. The wedding was exactly how I saw it in my dream in a beautiful church and her color was purple. I didn't know her. We stayed in a hotel that was similar to a log cabin. Tyra and I sat with his family. His mother said that she hopes that the marriage works out. I asked her why she said that. She said, because all these years all Jordan talked about was me. I assured her that it will work out.

• One night I had a dream about another friend. I dreamt that I went overseas to a great concert in a great hall. You had to wear gloves and a long dress and were seated on what appeared to be couches and little elegant café tables, where I was drinking sparkling apple cider out of a wine glass. The concert was starting, the lights dimmed, and there was Charles behind a round disc piano conducting and orchestra. The tickets were $100 per person and it was well worth it. The concert was phenomenal.

• I was at a crossroads in my life and I was asking God for direction. I prayed before I went to bed and I had a dream that night. There were three streets: one street was bright, the other was normal lighting, and the last was pitch black. I asked the Lord which street shall I travel. He said," Go to the pitched black street." I said to God," but God it is dark." He said, "you will be the light." He went on to say I am a vessel sort of like the candle cover. If He is not with me I will not be able to see at all, but if God is in me He will be the candle inside the candle cover and then I can light up

132

the street. I have Al B. Sure as a friend on FB. He went on Facebook Live talking about in these dark times we need to shine our light. He went on to say even if we don't feel like it, someone needs some light and it may be the only light they receive. Talk about a confirming word. I will shine my light.

• I had a dream that we (Fellowship Christian Church Worship Leaders) were at a leadership meeting with Bishop Thompkin..WE were doing an activity to show how well we work together. Everyone received packets at the beginning of the training, which had the materials you could use to work together.

Dora and Monet had a similar packet but mine was way different than theirs. Dora and Monet pulled their materials out, which connected with no problem. They looked at me as if to say, where are your materials? I was dumbfounded because mine were different not only in shape but in size.

I heard the Lord tell me to use what I was dealt. So we figured out how to connect my materials with theirs even though in our eyes it looked weird. Well, we won the challenge and were voted the most connected leadership team.

I stepped down from ministry. It was a rehearsal where I was leading worship. Dora said that Barbara was going to give harmony notes. This is what I have been doing whenever I taught songs. I agreed to let her do it, though I found it hard to do, because I bounce off of certain harmonies in order to lead worship effectively. Then I wanted to start a song at the last line of the song and was told by Barbara that I shouldn't do it because it wouldn't sound right. I felt my worship was being hindered. I could not worship God in spirit and in truth. It was controlled worship to me. I could not do it. I asked the head worship leader to have a meeting about the situation but it never happened.

I then spoke with Pastor Kathy. I explained that I felt like I was offering Barbara's worship unto God and I could not do that. It was never addressed, but I understand now that is where the church was at this time.

The dream did say that my path was different. Dora and Monet were still in the choir, and I was ministering outside of church. I guess that is why the Bible says that we are the church. I asked the Lord am I supposed to go back to the choir because it has been a year and the answer I received is, go where I tell you to go and do what I tell you to do…and my answer is Yes, Lord.

God is using me. I invited my friend Marnie to come to church and she came. The very next Sunday, Giana came with me to church. I have more time to minister to people God sends me more effectively. Now people I minister to, are finding their way to church. Thank you,,Jesus. I find myself like the bionic woman. God is making me bigger and better. Like Cameo sings, I am singing to God, I just want to be what you want me to be. God told me that my packet is always going to be different from the others but use what I am given and God will get the Glory.

My niece had good grades all her life worked hard to play ball and now committed to Syracuse. She goes straight into her destiny but me and my seed were dealt different cards…My son struggles with the academic part of school, but is an excellent ball player. He did not go straight into his destiny, having to take a different road because his packet is different.

My daughter struggles with anxiety because she learns differently. She is a slow starter when doing something new or when doing something that she doesn't think she is good at; different packet. I know great singers but my other daughter has a special "tone" added to her voice that makes you feel something. Her path is different, and so is her packet

My eldest gets jobs with no degree. She is so smart and can do anything she puts her mind to…She gets manager positions by sheer experience; different packet.

And my 2nd, she is the most intelligent talented lady I know but she still trying to learn how to walk. She gets along with no job because she is so gifted. Her packet, too, is different.

I learn differently. I remember in elementary school I had to take a program called SRA, because I did not read to understand. It was a program that put words together to make sentences and taught me how to read with clarity. In college, I was told by my college professor that I don't answer the question that is asked of me. I was told that I give a lot of information, sometimes information that one would not get out of the text at hand. She said she didn't know certain concepts were in the passage until I pointed them out, but I didn't answer the question. Learning differently was extremely frustrating growing up. I literally had to take it upon myself to find out how I learned, so I could tell the teachers and professors how I retained information. I got that honestly, because my father does that. I would ask him what color is the bottle. He would tell me that there was milk in the bottle, it has a nipple for the baby to drink out of, and that the bottle is round and it holds 8 ounces, but never got around to telling me what color it is.

I feel better reading a book from the bottom of the page to the top. A couple of my children also learn differently. I know that, because their struggles seem like what I went through while in school.

My daughter Tyra will not understand stuff, if you just stand there explaining for long periods of time. You have to show her several times and have her do hands on before she gets the information that you give her. They said Norman is not auditory at all. His information has to be written down step by step. Alicia needs to be tapping on something for her to learn. She knows how to do everything, but I think it's because she is more hands on as well. Artsy people have a hard time learning in a traditional class setting unless they are left brainers as well. My family and I definitely are set apart. Some people embrace our uniqueness and some are intimated by it.

People who learn differently presents a problem in school. We don't get teachings the traditional way. In fact, I noticed that whenever I explain to people about how we learn (specifically me and Tyra), they brush it off by saying things like everyone is like that...or I have the same problem or just have an answer for the information before the full information is presented, which just tells me that they don't understand us. We are different. For example, I do not have to record the song to get my part singing in the choir. If I do record, I will forget the part. Others have to record and study to memorize their part.

Tyra is an ABC learner. You have to teach her piece by piece. If she doesn't get A she is not going to get B and C. You have to make sure she has A, then she will give you A work. You also can't go too fast or if there are distractions, she is not going to get A. I have to admit her 10th grade team of teachers grasped on to her way of learning. Third quarter, she got straight A's and a favorable report card for fourth quarter. Our skill sets are tremendous.

I am not gassing myself up but I do speak several languages (introduction). Everyone one has a tendency to ask me questions because if I don't know the answer, I will find out. God gave me all these gifts so I can utilize them for the upbringing of his kingdom.

- I had a dream that I was hanging with certain church members. The rapture came and everyone I was hanging out with fell down into holes that were created. They were screaming for me to help them. I bent down to help one or all of them...I heard the lord tell me to get up. That was the second time I heard the Lord tell me to get up. I did, and then I saw the glory of God and several silhouettes. Then, I woke up and the sun was shining brightly through the window. Wow!

- I had a dream that I went to pay my mortgage at bank of America and all locations and ATMs were boarded up.

- I had a dream that there was a van parked at the corner of the street. Out came a bunch of guys with collared shirts and ties and clip boards. They were coming to see if anyone on the street wanted to sell their homes for top dollar. This dream reminded me of the movie Julia Roberts was in when the company was buying up people's property and making neighbors sick from their chemicals.

- I had a dream that one of my family members ended up in a one-bedroom cubby at a new YMCA. It was sort of a homeless shelter.

- I had a dream that I was standing in the middle of various language speakers and they all needed my help. They were all speaking in their native tongue to me at the same time. In sign language I asked everyone to stop talking. Then, I motioned for everyone to get in one line. They did, and then I started helping them one by one in their own native tongue. How awesome was that!

I wonder what language does my daughter Tyra speak.

- I had a dream about this other associate. I had a dream that though this guy was in church, he was not in church. There was a demon spirit standing in front of him and he didn't even try to get from spirits the control. He was director of music for a time. Though worship would be uplifting, he still stayed the same and then eventually left. For some reason, that demon spirit could not be shaken.

• I had a dream about Pastor Avril or Abril, what I call her. I had a dream that she was going to go solo after singing with the group, Archmont Hill. The kind of music that they sang kept Abril limited. She is currently on her solo journey, and the group retired Archmont Hill.

• I had a dream or should I say nightmare. The devil himself was standing in front of my children. He was causing them to talk back, smoke weed and the like…controlling them, if you will. I told him to give me my children back. I punched him like I was in a Marvel movie, because my fist became massive. He slammed onto the floor but no sooner than he dropped, came flying towards me, seeming to choke me and holding my mouth and nose closed and stared into my eyes as if to intimidate me. Even though he seemed to be choking me, I was still breathing just fine so I yelled "JESUS", and he disappeared. There is power in Jesus's name.

The question that I had though is how did he get so close? How could he have touched me?

I went on a fast for these answers. It turns out that sometimes I try to fight with my own strength; (pride). I took off my full armor of God, because I was caught off guard. I guess it's because I have a weakness for my children. The blood of Jesus will break all strongholds that is holding them captive…in Jesus name.

• Best weekend ever is when I dreamt about my wedding again. I also dreamt that Giana's singing the song we wrote and harmonized on called Come into My world. When I woke up the next day I was going to the movies with the

139

choir. I met up with Barbara. The bus we were supposed to take would have gotten us to Dedham late and we didn't want to miss the movie. We took another bus. The last stop for that bus, was right in front of Manhattan Bridal…We called an Uber that took too long to come, so we went into the bridal shop. We even picked the color of the brides-maids' dresses…then the Uber driver came. When we got in, the Uber driver asked which one of us was getting married. I answered so far, it's a dream. Driver said, we would not have a future without dreams…

The next day my friend Giana texted me saying that she was thinking of me and that song that we shared together. It was so amazing how the puzzle pieces were being put together and played out…

I have been dreaming a lot lately. I feel like Daniel in the bible. I dream of a lot of things. I dreamed that the Lord answered my question about why I haven't received a husband and why things are not going on as fast as I'd like; and he told me to trust the process and peace be my journey. If you are dreamer, ask the Lord to tell you what they mean. Do what Bishop Thompkin told me to do. Read Daniel in the Bible. Read about Joseph in the Bible. Pay attention.

And the Lord said to Paul in the night by a vision, "Do not be afraid any longer but go on speaking and do not be silent."

Acts 18:9

Speaking What I Wanna See

My son Norman is an NBA player. Right now, he is playing for the American Basketball Association, the New England Outta Towners. He is working. He was playing for college, but he left college ball. He knows how to dunk like no one's business.

My daughter Keala is a famous vocalist and psalmist. Currently, she is in a band called Jelani Sei and she has been in plays singing, dancing, and acting.

My other daughter Alicia is an entrepreneur. She will have her own business and it will be lucrative. This young lady knows how to do any and everything with the anointed hands of hers. I pray that she uses her gifts to God's glory

My baby Tyra is a great ball player and cook or whatever she wants to be, she is. She will not let fear be her crutch. She is currently in college and playing basketball. She gets every job that she interviews for. She has that *it factor*.

Tiana is a professional and great mom to her children. She will raise them up in the way they should go so that when they get old they will not depart from it. I want a better relationship with her.

I believe that my husband is coming. I even have my wedding planned out…the colors, the day of the week, and all. I will be married to the husband especially picked for me. He will love me up and I he. We will have each other's back. Of course, we will have fights but will decide to leave each other never. Oh, and my ring will have an orange tint in it.

I am a walking miracle. I know God is with me. He will never leave me or forsake me.

Miracles…

- They told me that I could not have children – I have five

- One day I was so sick. I felt like I was floating in the air. I saw myself laying on the bed. Then I woke up, almost like I died.

- Both Keala and I had/have breathing issues yet we sing.

- Had an operation on my vocal cords. Before surgery I sang Alto for thirty years. Now, I sing all parts.

- Speak Spanish – looks like I don't; in fact, I speak a little of several languages

- Bought a house working 30 hours with five children

- Walk 10,000 steps a day with a sore ankle

- My son Norman and daughter Tyra both had heart problems at birth & play basketball

These are some of my miracles. If you look at your life you will probably see miracles in your life as well.

Fellow Israelites, listen to this: Jesus of Nazareth was a man accredited by God to you by miracles, wonders and signs, which God did among you through him, as you your-selves know.

Acts 2:22

Crazy Things Happen

My life is like a whirlwind sometimes. There are so many times where things happen that you wouldn't believe happened except if I told you. Here are some of those things:

-I remember when we were going home from Shirley, ma. There were bugs up in the depot ceiling. When the train came in, it startled the bugs which caused them to start down towards us. When the train stopped, we ran into train. A lady that ran with us had on a wig...she snatched it off screaming and shaking it hard in front of the conductor who looked like he seen a ghost. That was so... funny.

-I was invited to my niece's wedding then uninvited a week before the wedding.

-Crazy start of the year 2018 but I know this is going to be a good year.

-I kicked all the kids out because everybody was trying to do their own thing. No one was being responsible or helpful. My motto is if you want to play you have to work hard. There was no work being done yet they wanted to play.

-Everyone came home and stepped up except one...the youngest one who insisted on being disrespectful. The house is now clean and everyone is working on self - maintenance

-Everyone left again and I was home by myself for months. It was the most reflecting time. It was same time that I had stepped down from the choir. I had more conversations with God that helped me more motivated than ever.

-There was one week where I did not see home. it was the week of Tyra's graduation. On Monday I went shopping for clothes for graduation. Tuesday, I went to my niece house to celebrate her birthday… Wednesday was a crazy day. I went to Brighton to get tickets for graduation and then I went to Cambridge but not before I picked up my sister's car. We went to Dorchester to get Tyra eyebrows done. we then went to pick up my niece from her school. I left them at my mom's then went to pick up my sister from work. We sent Tyra in an uber to her graduation. We piled up in my father's van to go to her graduation. After her graduation we went to eat at tri restaurant clear on the other side of town. That was all on Wednesday. By the time Thursday came, I had to take medication due the ankle swelling pain. So, I went to work then went to concert at nephew school. That Friday I went swimming. I was by myself because Tyra didn't show up and nor did my other swimming partners.

-Saturday was my daughter's birthdate so we went to buy decorations for Tyra graduation and then we bought my daughter a balloon for her birthday. We went to the nail shop and then went to a neighbor friend graduation party… by the time Monday came I wasn't going anywhere. It was a crazy week.

-One Monday, I did not get anything work done because fraud was running rampant. I received so many cases in one day, I was unable to start anything. Then when I got home, I had no keys, I left my keys in my coat I wore when it was cold along with the asthma pump. I asked Norman if he has his keys and he said no. Asked Alicia did she have her keys she said no. I was locked out. Alicia said that she was coming. I waited on the porch and waited and waited. Alicia came 1 ½ hours later. She jumped through the window and opened the door.

-One day, I was worshipping God while getting ready for work. When I got out of the bathroom and disrobed it was 7:13, my train comes at 7:32 and it is 7- minute walk down the street. I prayed and asked the Lord to help me to make sure that I catch the train. I proceeded on getting dressed. I tied my head put on boots which were difficult to put on and zipped a sweater that had the zipper on the side and walked swiftly down the street worshiping God. I looked at the time when I got on the train platform. It was 725. God heard my prayer and answered it.

I got to the train on time and with 7 minutes to spare before the train pulled into the station. God was pleased with my worship. He helped me catch train. Now I am going to worship Him because he is so good all the time and all the time God is good. I got to work and was filled with unspeakable joy. Though the day was crazy my joy cup was full. Praise is supposed to continually be in our mouths…gladly.

-One time my daughter got mad and started slamming things and left the house. Since she was under age I called the cops and they found her and brought her home. It was the craziest feeling when they brought her back and she is still fuming mad.

-The other day Tyra and I had two meetings. Since I didn't have a debit card due to fraudulent activity, we had to go to the bank to get money. We were down near the commuter rail...Tyra suggested we take the bus. We walked three blocks to the bus stop to find out the bus does not go to the mall until later so we had to run back to commuter rail. We made it. We went to the back and then got on the Silver slipper for breakfast. We were finished breakfast so we walked around Darby looking in the stores.

It was still too early so we walked down Washington street to Melrose Cass Blvd. to Tremlett Street by Ruggles Station and then to Millard Park. We were not sure what door to enter. We asked a security guard who told us that the office moved to the office building in Darby. We walked back down to Darby to find out that the office was at Millard Park.

We took the bus back and made it to our appointment. It was a very informative meeting. Then we walked Darby again to catch the bus to Kenmore. We had lunch then went to our second destination. It, too, was very informational and things looks promising regarding Tyra getting what she needs to graduate high school.

I walked down commonwealth avenue down Mass avenue to go to the train station to meet the keyboard player. I had to go to rehearsal. I got home at 10:30 or so that night.

-I then went to my sister's house but I could not walk a 10-minute walk which took me 25 mins because I was aching. My muscles were contracting and I am not sure why. Perhaps it was because I was on two high pressure meds and I took antibiotics for sinus issues. I stopped taking meds and the pain and stiffness went away.

-One day my colleague and I got on an extremely crowded train. there was this huge man who wanted to also get on the train. He just stepped in and pushed the people into the car with his stomach. The people fell into the train car like a wave. It reminded me of people being in a pool and a large man dives in and the people go flying every which way from the waves, lol. He just stood at the door holding on as if he did not do anything wrong. It was the funniest thing.

-At work, I was working on a big case with my boss and she asked me for some information, then I received an email from her boss asking for me to do something, my colleague was standing in my cubicle asking if I had a case, the other colleague was yelling to me asking for my phone number so that she can transfer a call to my line, one daughter was texting while the other was calling, then my work phone rang. This all happened at the exact same time. I was able to get back to each situation but didn't do any more work after that to regroup.

-I walked by a man dressed like Batman. He walked up to me and asked how I was doing and told me to be safe.

I say all this to say nothing ever comes easy for me I always have to jump hoops to get what I or my kids need. I couldn't make these occurrences up. Why is it that I have to yell and rant for my grown people to do what they are supposed to do? Did I teach them at?

Crazy moments are a constant in my life. Sometimes you just have to laugh

Leslie Guity

I wrote this poem about my crazy life.

Nothing ever comes easy for me. It goes a little something like this.

Nothing ever comes easy for me 1-30-01

Had to carry my transcript with me at RCC because their system kept aborting me

Had to fax a plan that UMASS faculty signed so that I can get my Bachelor's Degree

Had to speak to the North and East Zones to get my child into the Boston Public Schools

Had to call my job, Group Insurance Commission and the health insurance companies to find out what plan to choose.

Have 5 children and divorced and handling things singly

Thank God He doesn't give more than you can bear

Don't know where I'd be

Nothing ever comes easy for me.

This holds true always. I am always fighting for something.

Gifts And Challenges

I am discerning. I hear God tell me things about people. Some revelations God tells me to share with person and some revelations are just for me to pray for them and their circumstance.

At first, I didn't know how to handle my gift. I used to blurt out everything I heard from God.

I met this girl in Dunkin Donuts. She admired my earrings, so I gave her the business card of the person who makes them. Then I heard the Lord tell me that she needs to sing. I asked her if she sang.

She said no. She claimed her mom and uncle sings but she doesn't. There was a short pause then she said I used to sing but have had been through some trials and lost her passion to sing. I explained that praise should continually be in her mouth. Furthermore, I explained those trials she went through was a ploy to steal her praise and keep her silent but if you sing lives will be changed, people will be saved and most importantly you will be changed. She promised that she would sing in the morning and in the night. She will speak to the church choir about joining the choir. I told her if you don't remember anything else of our conversation remember not to let anyone or anything steal her joy peace or praise.

There was a lady at the café where I get my breakfast. I told her how great her shoes were. Then I asked her if she sang write poetry or writing a book, she said no. Then then asked me what church I went to . I told her I attend Fellowship Christian Church.   I asked her what church did she attend and she told me her church. I mentioned a person I know attends her church, told her that I used to sing with the person who is now at her church. She asked if I sang in my church. I told her that I am in my Esther year. God is working on me. I am trying to get books and songs out into the universe. I shared with her one of my songs. She then told me that she is the First Lady of her church.

They were taking long to cook my one egg and bacon perhaps for me and First Lady to finish sharing. I told her that I see books in her. She said that my discerning radar was on point because that was the third-time she heard it. She proceeded to tell me that she will make it happen.

We bid each other adieu and I went to work after finally receiving my breakfast.

I know when someone is pregnant. I know when someone is sick. I know when someone is withholding information. I know when death is upon someone. I know if people are having trouble in their relationship. I know when someone is around me without even seeing them. I have the ability to know when it is going to rain or snow and what time it is without wearing a watch.   I hear songs quotes and riddles all day long. I see poetry in my peripheral vision. I freak people out with my gifts. Sometimes I even freak myself out.

I spoke to with Bishop Thompkin about it before he was a bishop. He just told me to read the book of Daniel. I even spoke with Pastor Copper. No one gave me insight in how to use the powerful gift I possess. I sort of had to learn by hit or miss. As i matured I now know what to say and what not to say and what I should just pray for. Reading Daniel was helpful. I learned to discern my discernment.

I would like to meet another person that has this gift so we can learn trade stories on how to use this gift to bless and not to condemn. I am so glad that God gave me the gift to sing. I am so glad for my other gifts such as my gift of insight (prophesy). I was on fire this week. I knew that two women were pregnant before they even told me and they are not even showing…I even knew how tall this man was and that he didn't like to be that tall just by the way he walked.

I have a gift to comfort. I feel the need to make sure that people are okay when they lose some or when they are sick or during child birth. I will go to be by one's side no matter the time. I went to New York to visit my brother and a guy walked by us and I told my brother that the guy is in pain. He asked how did I know. I told him that I can feel his pain. He asked if I was a witch doctor. I told him no I am a child of God.

We have different gifts, according to the grace given to each of us. If your gift is prophesying, then prophesy in accordance with your faith. 7 if it is serving then serve; if it is teaching, then teach. 8 if it is to encourage, then give generosity, if it is to lead, do it diligently, if it' s to show mercy, do it cheerfully. Romans 12:6-8

Thank God for that gift even though I didn't even want it when I was growing up.

My mind wanders sometimes. I find it hard to finish project I start, i.e., this book. I have been writing this book for years. If I start to clean the living room and I find a dish and take it to the kitchen then I would start doing something in the kitchen forgetting I was cleaning the living room.

My friend told me a strategy; to put all the stuff that doesn't belong in the living room at the threshold until I finish then cleaning then put articles in their perspective places. This strategy works sometimes I forget the strategy though (shaking my head).

I smelled my daughter and I hadn't seen her in a week. An hour later she walked in the door.

I see choreography moves in my head for a song. I remember me and one of my daughter's choreographed a dance but we never had the privilege of sharing it.

I have ideas that will make a production be great.

This book is written how I think, which is that I have a tendency to jump all over the place with my ideas. This is also why it is taking me so long to write this book.

During a hospital visit there were eight lockers. I was adding the numbers crisscross then vertical putting number into sequence. I was told that it was the Fibonacci number theory. He was a mathematician. I was told that I have a mathematician brain...

That is wild. I remember numbers from telephone numbers to zip codes to people's social security number. That is crazy sometimes I wonder why I have all that information.

I still remember my first boyfriends phone number when I was a teenager ...

Songs poems, quotes, jokes are all coming out of my brain at the same time. Here are few quotes that I say all the time... I have my own language if you will:

Music is so powerful that a lullaby can put a baby to sleep...

I say things like, "Do the thing" and ask people "How you be"

When people are talking when I am talking, I say "Diarrhea of the mouth, constipation of the brain."

When people are sick, I always say, "Healing is yours or heal better or healing power." If someone loses someone I write, "peace and light..."

I text the kids "You good" to check to see if they are ok.

When someone say something that I don't like or make a joke about me I say "I don't like your attitude okay" or ah nah

Or if someone is making an excuse as to why they didn't do something that I tell them to "Save it for Oprah"

An Example Of The Riddles I Make

There is this guy who has been trying to get with me for years and I keep blowing him off. We go out to dinner to eat healthy foods and even have cheat days when we can have anything we want. He asked me for my hand and I would say yes. Then I would leave him standing at the altar. He would forgive me but then continue to ask again and again. Do know what his name is?

Gym …

Or sometimes it's about math story:

The man of means dated the math lady many times each time was greater...they even had pie until one day sumthing happened, they argued and he didn't like her additude. It was negative which put division between them. She had a word problem because she didn't know how to communicate. They needed to find a way to solve the problem.

I am always thinking. I have a tendency to make things:

The chandelier was so conceited because it always wanted to be the center of attention.

I am all about giving words of wisdom and encouragement:

Rejoice before result

A vase would not be a vase if it didn't go through fire. you are going to go through...but you will come out better

You do your part and let God do his…

If you prayed and gave something to God for him to handle, trust that God will do what he said he will do. Rejoice

The definition of the Me syndrome is when all you think about is yourself.

Don't be afraid to tell anyone that you don't know...you won't get to know what you don't know unless you communicate what you don't know and ask questions. Now once you ask the question and you get an answer you can't refute the answer because you didn't know the answer to begin with...knowledge is power.

Oh, how He loves you and me and our imperfection

Don't get comfortable in your current state...Grow...move forward

Just be you

I hope this book encourages you to get to know who you are. And if you want to know who you are, ask God the creator.

Nieces and Nephews

I love my nieces and nephews who are very creative smart talented and athletic. They will be great. My brother Rudolph has my niece Nora. She is ten weeks younger than my third daughter who went to college and worked 3 jobs at the same time and she graduated and still manages to go on vacations. My brother Renard has Anabelle, Anabella and Nabella. I affectionately call them the 3 belles. They are super intelligent. Their conversations are that of adults.

Then you have my sister Patrice's daughter Amarya who is a 6'4" with beauty and smarts and is currently a center of her college basketball team. She is studying to be an engineer. I am very proud of her. I dreamt about her playing for them. She likes my jokes.

You have my sister Tasha who has Martin, Elias and Tamar… They are like my kids …especially Tamar who I call CeeCee and she calls me Ceecee. Martin is cool like that. Martin made videos at a young age. He was also an entrepreneur at a young age. He would buy a box of fruit rolls and sell individual ones for a $1. Elias is so smart and a dancing machine. I remember when he was 3, I was watching him while his mother ran an errand and he saw a truck. He said "look at the Tonka truck with hydraulics." I didn't even know what a hydraulic was.

Ceecee's been singing since she was born. She was born prematurely…So nice to watch her grow up. She is absorbent. I love to teach her.

159

Then my sister Ronel's kids. She has Tara, Trenton and Trina who I call Grace. I heard the Lord tell me that God gave my sister Grace. Both Trenton and Trina play off of each other. They love to dance as well. Our parties always consist of dancing.

Forever Friends...

Do you have friends that are still in your life form 20 years or more? I do

I thank each and every one of them who has played a part in my life.

There is Giana who has been my friend since 6th grade. We may not see each other for years but then we will come back together as if there was no time lapse. She was there when my first daughter was born and when my last daughter was born. She is my first daughter's god mother. She comes when I need her. I don't even have to call her. It's like we get in touch with each other telepathically. One day my older daughter had to sing for the Governor. She told me last minute. I could not go because the other kids were sick and I didn't have any more leave. Giana came to save the day. She took my daughter for me.   this is one account in which she shows up and save the day.

There is a Sherry. She is also my oldest daughter's godmother. She went to RCC with me. She had me come to Florida to relax and release the pressures of everyday strug-gles. All I had to do is pay for my plane ticket and she took care of food and shelter and outings for me. I even came home with several pairs of her shoes with tags on it. Praise God for her.

There is Marissa. I met Marissa at church in foundations class 25 years ago. She is my daughter's god mother. Marissa lived with me until March 4. She had her baby on March 6 and I had mine on march 7. Because of her vast vocabulary, my vocabulary was improved because I had conversations with her. I had to literally look up the words she used.

When she lived me, I was watching a show on tv. I asked if she wanted to watch it with me. she said she doesn't feel like watching a bunch of white people running on the beach. One time she was trying to put her daughter in a program at church and they told her that it was full. Another lady walked up and they let her sign up. Marissa was fuming mad. I was speaking with my friend I call Doc and was trying to introduce Marissa to her. She said I'm sorry I'm bitter. Hi my name is Marissa…All of us started laughing.

There is also Linda Mia Margo Valerie and Marcia who are still my friends after many years.

I am blessed to have them in my life.

Greater love has no one than this: to lay down one's life for a friend.

John 15:13

The Re-Birth of My Creative Life

The Play

Since my children are grown, I started doing things that were in my heart. In 2017, a friend would see me on the train she would ask me to be in her play. I didn't answer her. She kept bumping into me and asking for me to be in her play. I finally gave in and said yes. I went to the rehearsal. I only wanted to sing in the choir. No lines, just in the choir. I sang alto… Kaeem was in the play and he said to me," I know you have a 9-5 job, but Leslie you were born for this theater life." Even though I didn't have lines to say I would act according to what the scene was about.

I was acting almost as if I have been doing it all my life. The last play that I had been in was in Elma Lewis days. I felt so comfortable on the stage. The play was a success and I met some great people from the playwright's church. The play opened up my creative doors. All of a sudden, more songs, ideas, poetry, and jokes etc., were coming into my mind like a flood.

The playwright wanted to change the name of the play. I asked her who gave her that name. She said God. I asked does she still want to change the name. She answered no.

I decided to be in the play again. This time, I was part of the planning of the play. I was part of the recruiter team.

163

I was recruiting everyone. I was assistant choir director for adults and children. I taught a piece of the choreography for the children's choir. I was basically the go- to person.

Before the play we had a gala to raise money and to promote the play. At the gala I was asked to model. The last time I modeled was at the Black Philanthropy as a child. He was going to put in this ugly outfit that didn't even compliment my body. I told him that I was not wearing what he picked out.

He told me to look around and I picked out an outfit. He claimed that he didn't have any accessories to go with the outfit. I told him yes, he does. He found accessories. I told him I need sunglasses. He again said that I did not need sunglasses. I told him if he wanted me to represent his store, I needed what I asked for. He then told me to pick a pair and I did. Then I went out there and modeled like a professional. I did get my expertise by watching American's next top model. I did the walk stop and pose twirl around walk backwards and all. The store manager had a big smile on his face. I was asked to do other modeling gigs after that. Some gala attendees came to the play.

Even the return cast had to audition. When I sang, the director and producer were looking at me like I had two heads. The director said that I was silent last year and I sing like that (he thought I was great). I am a worshipper.

Due to shortage of actors this year I sang soprano, played queen of Asia, and another part; and I actually had lines. It felt so good. I was in my element. There was talk about postponing the play until the next year but I told her that God wanted this play to happen. The show must go on.

This play bought all the folks whose talent was lying dormant out to create. I spent time with my grands because 3 out of 4 of them were in the play. Two were in the children's choir. They learned very quickly. Their schedule didn't allow them to come to many rehearsals, but they still jumped into their part as if they went to all the rehearsals. One was an acrobat. She was a natural as well, and she was never trained. I had to pick up my grandson from one end of the world, then picked the other girl from other end and the other in the middle, feed them, and still get to rehearsal.

One time my grandson had a food allergy and didn't perform that day but he managed to vomit all over the men's bathroom, ceiling and all. It was wild!

The show despite all the lumps and bumps, up and downs was a great success Our rehearsals were like a whirlwind due to attitude issues but it was just like a vase has to go through fire to become a vase so did the play. God was all in it.

Music Language Refresher

My friend has been going to a music convention for years and I could not attend because of family obligations. This year I attended because my children are young adults now. I am so glad I went. It was nice sing alto in a choir. I haven't been singing at church because I am being obedient to the Lord trying to utilized other talents that he bestowed upon me. I met new people that live in different parts of United States. I listened to some powerhouse singers and go a rhema word from God form gospel greats such as Marvin Sapp. I even attended two workshops: SongWriting and Book Writing and Publishing, and was truly enlightened.

Attending this convention also gave me ideas on how to get streams of income not just living check to check which I have been doing for the better part of my life. I am even thinking about owning my own company, which would consist of teaching voice, self-esteem, selling my books, production work, etc.

Everyone Has Areas To Work On And Here Are Mine

I want to be more approachable for a relationship. I have a tendency to run away when an individual gets close too fast.

Help me to speak positivity so prospective husband can feel respected

Help me to make sure that my house is filled with treasures and not bitterness and loneliness.

To practice what I preach

Funny part is I keep telling my son stop doing just enough to pass and I have been doing the very thing I told not to do all my life regarding my finances...

I don't get mad often but when I do it's nothing nice. I'm working on angering but sinning not.

Smh...I always tell everyone to breathe in through their nose and out through their mouth, yet I hold my breath when I walk up the stairs unconscientiously.

I am working on keeping focused, which is hard because my mind is always wondering.

I want to complete goals that I set and not take forever to accomplish them.

What are areas do you need to work on? Strive to be a better you!

I have to check myself because I noticed that a lot of people i.e., the general manager at the bowling alley, my colleague, and then my co choir member tried to demean me. Am I handling these situations as Jesus would? Sometimes I avoid conflict situations and then get reprimanded when I do deal with them. I am still learning my real self. My colleague, who I checked when he tried to tell me what to do, no longer speaks to me. One day, my other colleague that he asks questions to, was out, and he was forced to speak with me. That was funny. God keeps you from dangers seen and unseen. I am glad he doesn't talk with me because he would probably speak to me so condescendingly.

When you know that God's glory is being revealed through you

When I cross the street on a green light both sides stopped like I parted the red sea

When I walk by, the birds do not fly away

When babies who don't normally go to people, go to you

When you are sitting at your desk and co-workers come to your desk for Godly advice

When directors who are leaving come bid you good-bye, when they leave the agency

When someone contacts you and asks you if they can accompany you to church.

*When you visit people house who has a dog/cat and their
pet comes and sits next to you.*

As I was on the bus, a drunk man got on and walked
to me and said you are a woman of God can you pray for me.
I didn't hesitate, I placed my hands on him and prayed for
him. He thanked me. He said that I am wise and asked my
age. I told him that I was 25 years old. He laughed. He told
me that he prays daily to keep him safe and that he even
prays for his mother and brother. He said he did not know
how to pray. I said that prayer is a conversation with God. It
doesn't not have to elaborate like he said my prayer was,
God knows his heart. Though he had his problems he had
manners he was trying to give his seat to a lady and he
couldn't barely stand. In fact, I prayed for the whole bus.
Thank you for using me, God. It is great that people can see
the God in me. We are called to be salt and light and to make
a difference in the world.

Benefits Of Walking Your Walk With God

The shuttle ride for the commuter rail was supposed to drop me at the designated station asked me where would I like to be dropped off. He said that he is at my service. He dropped me off at my destination.

The uber was 3 dollars to get home. When I came down to get it the uber, the driver was standing outside an open door waiting for me to get in. And when he was dropping me home, he came and opened the door and put his hand out to help me out of the car.

I very seldom do I have to open a door. Someone will always seem to come and open the doors for me. Especially when I have my hands full.

One day I declared a fast because I needed some answers to some questions that I have been wrestling with. I went to the café I usually buy breakfast from to get tea. There was a drunk lady sitting at one of the tables. Before I could get to the counter the lady said "remember you are fasting. Then everyone that was there starting a conversation about fasting. I did not know that lady. Every day after that day whenever I went to get tea clerk will ask me if I am still on a fast.

I was told that I dress like a work of art. Great compliment but it's the God in me. I am constantly being gifted scarves earrings glasses. It is not me they see but the God in me.

When I ask God to help me find something. I find it.

The other morning, I was looking for a specific pair of earrings to go with my outfit of that day. I store it in a large bag. I looked through the bag 3 times. I then asked God for the earring. I closed the bag. When I picked up the bag the other earring was on the floor.

I am a recovering hoarder. I have papers everywhere. I asked the Lord where is a specific document. I already looked everywhere I thought it might be to avail. I will hear a still small voice tell me to look through a pile of papers and eureka.

Sing

Failed relationships and two baby daddies, single parenting and I am still standing because I sing praises to the Almighty. The first music notes were the heartbeat. Where would this world be without music? It would be boring I tell you that.

I learned scripture that has gotten me through life's struggle through songs. *2 Chronicles 7:14 If my people who are called by my name will humble themselves and pray...and seek my face turn from their wicked ways. And will I hear from heaven, forgive thy sins and heal thy land... if my people will humble themselves and pray.*

John 3:16   God so loved the world that he gave his only begotten son and whosoever believeth in him shall not perish shall not perish but he shall have he shall have everlasting life I learned these songs before I gave my life to Christ.

Music and singing helps me through my day. Singing and music helps me through life trials and triumphs. I don't know where I would be without music.

I am a worshipper. Worshippers are the front line in God's army. Let's worship HIM in spirit and in truth. The importance of worship. It is a weapon. I was created to worship...ready for battle. When I worship God, I want the people to feel HIS presence in the room

Music joins people together. People should learn from music. Everyone is playing together to make beautiful music. This should be family. This should be relational.

You hear music everywhere. I always ask how would this world be if it were Musicless?. Pretty dull, huh. Just think, there would be no music videos; the movies were just be a mono or dialogue. There would be no elevator music. One Life to Live would just be one life to live. There is a song for everything.

While waiting on the train, there were times when I felt like singing out loud. I felt like worshipping God right there, because God is so… awesome!

It doesn't matter the genre of music, whether it be Classical Rock, Contemporary, Gospel, R&B or Rap. There is a message in the music.

During slavery time they sang while doing work. Some songs were code telling people where to go to escape. Music is a part of history and our culture.

My parents are Garifuna people. The language they speak is similar to French and that of the Mayan Indians. Their culture consists of dancing "punta" and singing and playing drums.

Music is a language that God used to speak to me, to guide me through life's ups and downs. Health issues, racism, single parenting, mental abuse and rejection, were all dealt with through song, worship and praise through music.

Music is embedded in my soul

Why do they have music therapy? It is because music is powerful; it is healing. When I sing, I forget about my problems. When I worship God, I feel like I am flying; like there is nothing that I cannot do because that is my way of fighting for my life.

In the Bible Paul and Silas were praying and singing hymns and all of the sudden the prison doors swung open. Acts 16: 25-26

Jehoshaphat appointed men to sing to the Lord and to praise him ahead of the army saying Give thanks to the Lord, for his love endures forever... and the Lord set ambushes against the men who were invading Judah and they were defeated... *2 Chronicles 20:22*

As I sit here writing this book, I am listening to worship music. I know without a doubt that God has my back and that no weapon formed against me shall prosper. That is why it is so important to watch what you are listening to.

Music makes you family. If we were a band and are all are not in agreement and doing our own thing, it would be noise, but when we decided to play together on one accord or in harmony, then there would be beautiful music played. That is how family is supposed to be. Everyone is different in their own right but puts in their part in the family and it will be beautiful music.

Speaking of music…I went to a show that my daughter was in. This is the same daughter that told me that she would never sing again; the same daughter that was saved and led worship at her church, and sang a Donny Hathaway song and rocked it. She was amazing…everything truly goes full circle and she has a testimony. That shows how fear can keep you from your true destiny if you let it. Her testimony also shows that the prayers of the righteous truly does availeth much.

Her singing reminds me that there is a God and that he did it for her that he can do it for all my children who are sitting on their gifts not showing the world who they really are and how dangerous they are. Her testimony also made me realize that I did the same thing she did for the longest time.

Today I endeavor to sing, to write new songs. I will sing when I am happy, sing when I am sad, sing when I am going through, sickness…whatever the situation *I will sing*.

As a matter of fact, those who are going through on Facebook, that I know I sing, I tell to sing.

I now know I am a daughter of Abraham. I walk in divine health and wholeness. Every morning new mercies I see and I walk intentionally by faith. Singing is medicine for the singer and audience. Worshipping opens hearts to hear a word from God. Singing is breathing; breathing is singing.

I have been happy these days. Music is pouring out of me like rivers of living water. I see things differently now. I know that my family will be saved …I know that I will be married on a Wednesday. I know that God will give me what he promised. I have someone helping to get the music that I hear get out of my head finally. I felt constipated. Many told me that they would help me with my music but did not. I will continue to find a way to get my music out.

Every time I go through something, I pray to God about it and He asks me "Do you trust me?" I say yes. Then I worship God with all of my heart and soul. All the energy that I would use worrying, I use to worship God and therefore usher people into God's presence. I was leading worship and doing worship videos on Facebook. Use me Lord after thine will.

I am excited for how God is going to move. Though everything looked like it was going awry I can still see the flowers through the trees. I am learning to not look at situations as bad because God works everything out for our good. Romans 8:28 therefore, I rejoice.

God is definitely getting me ready for something better. He is showing me something I would never see in my natural eyes. I am so grateful that God loves me in spite of myself. Loving God is teaching me how to love. I never really knew what it was. I never even experienced it. I ask God to teach me your ways oh Lord...Teach me how to love like you love. And, He is teaching me...I am sitting at his feet eager to learn how to be like HIM.

All I want to do sing praises to Jesus. He is the King of Kings and Lord of Lords...Hallelujah!

God is actually talking to me through each situation I went through in my life. Maybe he allowed hurtful things to happen so I won't have any excuse to not finish my resume or write in my book. The Prophetess did tell me that I need to finish my book.

The song poet says, when the praises go up blessings come down. I have been truly blessed despite all that I have been through.

I am on a verge of a breakthrough and I decided to look up scriptures regarding breakthrough in the Bible. Google brought me to 2 Corinthians 5:20 which say that David went to Baal Perazim and God allowed David and the army to defeat the Phillistines…The place signified that the Lord bursted out or breakthrough …I couldn't pronounce the word Perazim except to say Praise Him. I started jumping at the thought of just Praise God and your breakthrough will come.

NO Matter what I have been going through, I still find it in my soul to Praise the Lord with all I've got.

Music Has Power (2/16/2016)

The only rap I want to hear is the unwrapping of a candy wrapper, so silence take a nap rapper

I like to hear classical jazz and old skool rock to me sometimes a little odd

The best thing I like to sing is gospel with my hands raised high singing my praise to

Almighty God.

Music has power don't say its only music because that's where you've gone wrong

You know music can make you think about love or hate depending on the song.

One song poet says music makes you lose control, when we worship God we show people that God is in control

The devil wants to kill steal and destroy us and you, it doesn't matter whether young or old

That's why there is a bunch of worldly music where millions of platinum albums are being sold Singing and rapping everything from you do what you feel like doing fornication and sleeping with someone 's wife

We need to sing and make more songs about Christ you give your life

You are hearing everything from swearing and smoking weed and not enough about you being Abraham's seed

Jesus on the cross He bleeds to set us sinners free.

Elevator music is played to ease your mind, Music played in the mall making you think its shopping time.

Songs like No air, no air tell us that you would die without men

But Gospel music says you can't afford to live without HIM

And spreading the word and the love of Jesus So.. we need to worship and praise Him so he can stay next to us

Just because I am speaking truth, don't get your face all sour

All I'm trying to say is that, Music Has Power!

I'll praise the Lord at all times. God will amaze

I Have Written Songs Before Christ As Well As After...*Music Is How God Speaks To Me.*

He has been speaking to me my whole life.

I sang at Ray Flynn's inauguration when he was becoming mayor of the City of Boston, I sang when Nelson Mandela came to Boston. I sang in a program called Metro Pathways. I got the opportunity to sing in the All City Choir and we met in the Boston School Department building. I also sang in the choir where we sang down the cape and slept in a wood cabin.

I sang in Black Nativity ... There was time where the whole family sang in it and my second child Alicia played Jesus while her sister's father played Joseph. I sang with Kuumba, Harvard University's choir. I even sang on Community Auditions with Dave Maynard. When he asked what did I want to be when I grow up, I said a singing secretary. I am sort of that right now...funny.

Singing took me everywhere. When I sing it makes me feel like I have wings to fly. I would be taken out of class to do concerts. What a blessing God gave me to be able to sing. God told me that he would be depositing songs in my heart. He started depositing so many of them in fragments

183

that I had to stop singing other people's songs. I have to constantly carry a recorder so I can sing into it. I can't wait until I can get someone to help me put the song pieces together.

My daughter Keala helped me put one song together and my brother is supposed to help me with the others. We shall see what God has in store.

We were told that we can record our original works with one of the choir member's connections. I also got in a reverend's Uber who says he does music and has a studio at his church. He said that I can use his church when I start making my music. God is so good. There are always open doors of opportunities. This encounter was a set up. I was already done Christmas shopping and one of my friends asked me where I was. She had just gotten to the shopping center and she wanted me to hang with her. I shopped with her for two stores and when she was going to her third store, I bailed out and got in the reverend's Uber. How about if I hadn't hung out with her and left when I was done shopping. Would I have gotten into his uber?

Music Lives In Me

When writing a song, I not only hear the words, I hear trumpets, cymbals, violins, etc.

If I only learned how to play an instrument effectively, I would have had the songs out already. Everything will happen in its time.

This scripture comes to mind...*He put a new song in my mouth, a song of praise to our God. Many will see and fear, and put their trust in the Lord...Psalm 40:3*

I sing through everything...

When I was in KUUMBA, Harvard's university's choir, they needed someone to sing during intermission. I was asked if I know how to sight read. I answered sort of...I was given a hymn book and told to sing ...I learned a new hymn that day with my limited sight- reading skill. Kuumba means creativity.

When ministering at Jubilee one day we went to evening prayer and we were praying way in the back. Next thing you know it, we were given mics and was told to pick a part.

Even at baptism I was asked to minister. I was supposed to have one keyboard player then another showed up and I didn't even know him. I was singing one song and he changed the song mid singing because I kept on stumbling over the words in the chorus. He said, yea you know this song. My son was calling. I answered, so the boy could hear that I was singing. He kept calling me when the keyboard player said," what dem critters want?" The pastor of the hour started singing an unfamiliar song. Me and the keyboard player looked at each and shrugged. He told the Pastor we don't know that song, you are on your own pastor, lol. I wonder if the baptismal candidates knew that we were laughing the whole time. When baptism was over, I called my son and asked him what he wanted. He said" May I have some popcorn?" We were laughing even harder.

At several weddings the bride would change her song 20 times before telling me which song she selected. The song they chose I wouldn't know by heart...I had to ask the Lord to minister the song for me. What is good, is that God always sends the holy spirit to sing for me. Singing and worshipping is like painting on a canvas. You stroke each note like each line on a painting. I want to paint a beautiful picture unto the Lord.

I went into an art gallery. I love art (paintings, cards, jewelry, bags). The artist showed me her paintings. She said that she was inspired by nature. They were beautiful. She then asked me to show her my artistry. So, I sang *You are Holy by Lisa Mcclendon*. She was staring in awe as I sang each note.

After I was done, she asked for a hug. We hugged. As I left, I still had a lot of time to spare before rehearsal. I stopped by the nail shop and got a manicure. Then I went to rehearsal. God moves when you worship. Something happens when you sing. You have oil and power. You can take back what the enemy has stolen.

It seems that every sermon that I have been listening to says Praise God...If you want a breakthrough, Worship God. Looking back at my life I realize that God has been with me all along and is still with me. Through thick and thin he guides he loves he comforts he is peace in my life.

Everyone has an outlet for them to use to keep from pulling their hair out during life's ups and downs. Like I said, for me it is to sing; to worship God with everything I've got.

You have read a glimpse of my life journey and if you were confused in any way, or thought my life was crazy...you would be correct. Singing always seems to bring my spirits up and bring me to a place of peace, where I am able to think about the goodness of God and how he is/was able to bring me through many trials and tribulations. Yet, I am still standing.

God has given everyone gifts and talents purpose and dreams. The anecdote to anxiety and depression is to find out what your passionate about and do it, and to find out what your purpose is and fulfill it. If you dance, dance. If you draw, draw. If you paint, paint. If you sing, sing. Do not be afraid to shine your light. If you are, take one step at a time to your purpose. If you are opening a business, think of a name and name it. Get it copyrighted. Write a business plan.

If you want to know love, seek God for he is love. You have to have faith for without it, it is impossible to please God. You will have trials and some will feel like you won't make it...Pray and ask God for guidance. He speaks every day.

Sure, I freak out sometimes because I am human, but know that God will not leave you or forsake you. He wants us to have hope and a future. After the play that I was in opened up my creativity door, I have never been happier.

Find out what makes you tick. Love yourself. Seek first the kingdom of God and everything else will be added. During hard times and crazy days do your passion. I feel like I have been re-born and that I am just starting to learn how to walk in this creative light.

I have big ticket items in front of me i.e., I have to pay taxes for the first time in my life., I had a large dental bill and God took care of it. I have the kid's student loans and home repairs. God fixed and is fixing it. Had a boiler problem, car problem and car remote problem, I knew God who loves me would supply all my needs. Nothing is too hard for him. Therefore, I will praise and worship HIM -

Music Is The Key!

Now to him who is able to do immeasurably more than all we ask or imagine, according to his power that is at work within us.

Ephesians 3:20

Music is the Key

Man,

Music is the Key

For music lives deep within me

All instruments playing

Shhh… listen to the snare drums

I'm Overcome

By the steady rhythm that you hear

Of your heart beat when you see someone who you

Hold dear

Music is relationships

From beautiful love songs to someone did somebody wrong

Song to the praise

And worship songs from the baby lullaby

To the songs you sing when people die

For if it weren't for music

Slavery would not have been taken

Would have thought God had forsaken

Overworked our bodies were achin'

What a rude awakenin'

Man,

Music is the key

Sometimes problems follow me

Need something to give release

Man music is the key

Sounds of music soothes the average beast

Gives them peace

People play music in their cars

There is music played

In the local bars

If you sit quietly you will hear a song playing

From a distance

A song for every situation

For every circumstance

They play music everywhere

Like on a plane

While in the air

Music Is The Key

When you are on hold on a business line

On law and order when one commits a crime

There are songs you just sing

Songs you dance to,

Rap to, romance to hmm

Music is used to usher people into the presence of

The Lord

Bring people on one accord

Rest assured

With music, everything will be okay

Helps to get you through a crazy day

Therefore, play music, make music and we shall all agree

Music is the key man.

When I need to write songs, I ask the Lord what the words and the melody will be.

Through my entire life Music, Singing and Worship kept me whole.

No matter what you are going through, what kind of trouble you are in, or what battle you are fighting, send praise out first... Love Deeply and Sing until your last note...

About The Author

Leslie Guity is a Boston Native, and a first generation Honduran American. She is a vocalist and vocal instructor (individuals, children and adult choirs) whose versatility include acting, choreography, theatre production and modeling. She attended The Elma Lewis School of Fine Arts in her youth which has shaped her and her artistry. She sang for the Mayor's inauguration in 1983 and for Nelson Mandela during his visit to Roxbury, Ma. She sang in many local choirs including Harvard University's choir, KUUMBA. Leslie had, at times lessened her pursuit of her aspirations, in order to raise her five beautiful children. She is also, an aspiring songwriter, poet, and now a freshman author. She has begun a new chapter in her life pursuing the arts. She endeavors to shine her light with her God given gifts.